SECRET OF THE MARTIANS

By
PAUL W. FAIRMAN

ARMCHAIR FICTION
PO Box 4369, Medford, Oregon   97501-0168

WERE MARTIANS REALLY DANGEROUS?

No human being on Earth or Mars seemed to think so. Very few of the human colonists had ever even seen a Martian. Indeed, the Martians had essentially given way to Terran colonists centuries before and allowed them to have all the equatorial regions of the planet for farming and other human endeavors. The Martians themselves retreated to the northern countries near the polar ice cap. There they had lived in isolation for many generations.

But then one day the slain body of a Terran botanist was found. When a security agent from Earth was sent in to investigate, he found himself in a web of interplanetary conspiracy that threatened the existence of every human being on Mars, and possibly Earth itself.

FOR A COMPLETE SECOND NOVEL, TURN TO PAGE 87

CAST OF CHARACTERS

REX TATE
He was strong enough to snap a man's spine with his bare hands, and weak enough to succumb to a dark-haired beauty.

JEAN WILKS
She was beautiful and courageous, but could those qualities save her from certain death at the hands of Martian extremists?

TOMMY WILKS
It's not many 15-year-old Earth kids that end up on Mars with a Martian friend and a diary filled with incredible deeds.

PANDEK
His hatred of Terrans had transformed him into a revolutionary killer with a desire to wipe out every human being on Mars!

MAXIS
Loyal to the rightful Martian ruler to the very last, he was the only hope of saving his race from sure destruction.

FANTON
This benevolent Martian ruler was very old and near death. Only the greatest scientific secret of the solar system could save him.

GORDON MALLOY
As Chief of Interplanetary Security, it was his job to send men on dangerous missions, even if it might mean their deaths.

CHAPTER ONE

GORDON Malloy, Chief of Interplanetary Security, rocked back in his chair, and with seeming unconcern looked Rex Tate over searchingly. "How was Pluto?"

"Stinking. Why we want that frozen lump in the Federation is something I can't figure."

"Rich in minerals."

"You left me there for seven Terran months," Rex allowed criticism to sound in his voice.

This did not bother Malloy. "Good for you. Toughened you up. Safe too. Never much trouble on Pluto."

"That's why I joined up. So I'd be nice and safe."

"I've got something in mind for you."

"Where?"

"Mars. But it could be nasty so you'd better go back to Pluto."

"Try and get me on a ship. What's with Mars?"

Malloy looked for a place to put his feet and found only the top of his desk. Up there they looked like a pair of crossed banjo cases.

"I wish I knew."

"I'll go find out for you."

Malloy's eyes brooded. "The thing started as a result of privileges and stupidity, the way most things of this sort do. As you know, Mars is the only planet in the Federation without representation because the Martians refused to represent themselves. They wanted no part of the alliance." Malloy glanced up quickly. "How's your knowledge of the Martian background?"

"Sketchy. Ask me about Venus, Mercury, Neptune, Pluto. By all means ask me about Pluto."

"We're talking about Mars. When we went up there in 2091, we found as close to a dead planet as you could want. There were people, but damned funny ones. They wouldn't fight us or they wouldn't join us. They had a kind of pride we've never been able to analyze. They just kept backing away.

"We found rich minerals and fine farmland—land that had lain fallow for ages just waiting for the plow. And plenty of water. Every spring, the ice cliffs at the poles melted on schedule and sent down the moisture for bumper crops.

"But the Martians didn't farm—they didn't mine— they didn't do anything so far as we could discover except back away into their caves and rocky fastnesses up north and give us the cold eye."

Rex knew all this but he liked to hear The Chief talk—liked to be with him, as did every other agent in the Gang, so he registered bright interest and listened.

"They rebuffed all our advances and so we let them alone."

"But that happened on other planets too," Rex said innocently, "and so we went right in and got acquainted—looked in their bedrooms and their dresser drawers."

Malloy frowned slightly. "But on Mars, we didn't."

"Nope. I wonder if it could have been because we had their land and their mines and didn't think they had anything of value around their north pole?"

"You're speaking disrespectfully of the System," Malloy said in mild disapproval. "You sound as though you think we moved in and took planets over. All we did was develop latent resources—"

"—Make for the better life—"

"—Invite them to join us for a greater System—"

"—The same way the British and the Dutch and the French and the Russians did in ancient times here on Terra."

MALLOY regarded his big feet with hostility, as though they and not Rex Tate had been speaking. "Do you want this assignment, or don't you?"

"Sure I want it." Rex grinned. What other department chief would let a subordinate sound off? None except Malloy. That was one of the things that made up for the low pay.

"All right—then shut your trap and listen. As I said, the Martians backed off into those hills and caves and hung out a *Private* sign that we respected for three hundred years. Then, about six months ago, a Martologist named Spencer got tired of testing flora and fauna in the safe areas and wangled a permit to penetrate the taboo areas around the pole."

Rex Tate straightened—honestly amazed. "Alone?"

"No. In the company of his twenty-year-old daughter."

"Why we wouldn't even send a nuclear battalion in there! Who issued such an insane permit?"

"That's not our business. The criminally stupid ass is being hunted from other directions, but in this age of red tape and buck-passing I doubt if he'll ever be found. Our job lies elsewhere. We've got to find out what happened to Spencer's daughter."

"What about Spencer?"

"He came back."

"Without his daughter?"

"Yes."

"I'd like to talk to the slob for a few minutes."

Malloy dropped his feet to the floor. "Come on. I'll give you a chance."

Rex followed Malloy out of the office. They got on an elevator that dropped them to a sub-basement. Malloy manned a scooter and they rode for several minutes down a long, straight corridor.

Just when Rex wondered whether or not The Chief knew where he was going, Malloy stopped the scooter in front of a closed door. He opened the door and motioned Rex inside.

The room was small and bare, boasting as furniture, only a rectangular table in its center. On the table sat a rectangular box. Malloy pointed into the box and said. "All right—start talking."

A small chill danced down Rex's spine. In the box lay a serene-faced, middle-aged man with his hands folded over his chest. He had a rosy complexion and appeared to be napping. What an odd place for a man to sleep, Rex thought. He glanced up at Malloy. The latter said, "As near as we can tell, he's been dead for four months."

"But—"

"I know. Perfectly preserved—the skin soft—all normal fluid still present in the body. Nothing's wrong with him except that he's dead."

Rex touched the soft tissue. It was cool. "How can you figure the time?"

"He came in on a food freighter—in a cargo of potatoes that was sent from a farmer's market at a place called New Iowa in the heart of the Martian farm belt."

"Not far from the forbidden polar circle," Rex said.

"I thought you didn't know anything about Mars."

"When things were dull on Pluto, I studied timetables."

"That's interesting. I'll issue them to all agents."

"Of course you've got no proof that the body was put aboard at Iowa."

"Yes we have. The hold was locked and sealed there. The body was inside. The seal was unbroken."

The closed eyes of Professor Spencer made Rex almost as uncomfortable as the closed lips. "All right. I've got the picture. What do we do? Send in a battalion to question the Martian taste in gift packages?"

"We've got no proof the Martians did this."

"Who else?"

"Maybe some transplanted Terran farmer took up taxidermy on the side."

"The odds are way against it."

"So are the odds against a solar eclipse, but they happen."

"Then we make no hostile gestures?"

"Not until we know the score. That's what I want you to do, Rex—go out to Mars and find the score."

9

"Okay, Chief." Rex took a last look at the body. "And if I come back in that shape, check my pockets. There might be time to write a note."

"Don't be such a pessimist," Malloy growled.

*   *   *

(From the diary of Tommy Wilks)

The first thing you miss on Mars is the green. The things hardest to get used to are the reds and the yellows and the tired browns. Never is there any bright rich green filled with the promise of spring as I grew used to in Kentucky back on Terra. Because this is a dying planet and even when the Martian spring does come, there is a feeling of tiredness in the air.

And the warm rain on your face. You miss that too because there is no rain on Mars. You keep looking at the sky, hunting for the big black thunderheads that sent people running for cover back in Kentucky. You look and look until your eyes ache and even the sting of icy cold rain would be nice.

The water here is all underground and in the canals. It is good water, running down through the bogs and the rivers and the marshes in spring when the big northern ice cliffs melt.

It is very funny about the ice cliffs. Up there it snows in the winter I guess because they get higher and higher until they are like mountains. Then, in spring, they melt in a few days. Nobody knows much about the ice mountains because they are in the middle of the forbidden polar zone. It is said there are Martian people up in the forbidden circle but I don't think so. Because why would anybody live in such a place when the level lands and the old sea bottoms and the canals are down here?

Anyhow, we never go there. The only Martians I ever saw are the ones that come by like tramps asking for food. We always give it to them because they are always hungry and we don't want any trouble. And then there is Barzoo. He was here when we came. He lives in a little stone house out beyond the potato fields. All Martians have hard brown skins—almost like shells—and instead of white in their eyes, like Terrans, they have light green, and the pupils are always jet black. Looking at a Martian is a little hard to get used to at first but after while it's all right.

Dad and Mom made me stay away from Barzoo at first, but he was harmless and now they let me visit him. We talk but I can only understand a little of what he says and he can't understand much Terran. He is a funny man, Barzoo. He never smiles and gives you the idea he has only contempt for Terrans. But he takes me and shows me where the big gadfish hide in holes in the canals and how to catch them with a white pebble on the end of a line.

Nobody minds Barzoo.

I am Thomas Wilks Junior, but everybody calls me Tommy. I am fifteen years old and I like to write and someday I will go to Terra to some big university and learn to do it well and then I will write stories all about Mars for the Terrans to read.

My father is Thomas Wilks Senior. My mother is Lucy Wilks. My sister is Jean Wilks. Father brought us to Mars when the Federation opened this land. It is very easy to grow good crops here—very big potatoes—because Dad says ages ago it was farmed by the Martians and the fields and the canals are all here. We put the potatoes on big space freighters that take them back to Terra. All the farmers send their potatoes in the big freighters and they all talk about going back themselves after they get rich out here but I have a feeling very few of them will go. There is something *about this planet that grows on you. It's awfully cold a lot of the time and you have to learn to walk carefully or you go right up in the air. But you get used to it. And two moons instead of one.*

I like keeping a diary because someday I will need what I'm writing now for my stories about Mars and will become very famous and live in a high tower in Kentucky. Or maybe I will build a tower right here on Mars.

* * *

(Wednesday)

We have a new man working for us. He came in on the last freighter. He is very tall and has yellow hair and he is different from most men that come here to work. Most of them go to the saloon when the ship sets down, but this one went to the candy store and that was where I met him.

He bought me some ice cream and we talked about Mars. I guess I did most of the talking. I told him all about the farm and about Barzoo and the gadfish you catch with a pebble. He seemed very interested in Barzoo and said he'd like to meet him.

I told him if he worked for Dad I would introduce him to Barzoo and he said all right. Which Dad slapped me on the back for later because help is hard to get and he gave me credit for talking the yellow haired man into working for us.

His name is Rex Tate and we didn't ask him how he happened to come out here. We're just glad that he did because help is a problem.

After this I guess the farmers will check the candy store too when they come into Iowa along with the saloon. But who would expect to find a grown man like Rex Tate in a candy store? He's different than the other workers who come here. A lot more intelligent. I like to talk.

CHAPTER TWO

REX Tate, clad in a Martian fox jacket against the sharp winter air, worked at a strand of broken fence on the far north line of the Wilks farm.

He straightened and looked off across the dull brown plains. The experts said this had all been ocean once; back in the days when Terra was a seething, untenanted ball of hot lava. Rex wondered how right they were.

One thing was sure. A no more dull, drab, peaceful landscape could possibly be imagined. He turned to look northward toward the high ice cliffs of the polar circle. The thin air made distances deceptive and the cliffs looked to be hanging almost over Rex's head. But he knew they were many miles away.

He frowned. This had seemed the logical place to start his investigation, yet what evil could lurk among these simple energetic Terrans. Such an act as had been perpetrated upon Professor Spencer was certainly beyond their ability to conceive, and Margo Spencer was certainly not hidden among them.

Only one thing kept him in this vicinity and it was indeed a frail thread. The Martian hermit young Wilks had told him about. He wanted to look the man over but had delayed, feeling that even though the lead seemed hardly to be taken seriously, caution was still the better part of wisdom.

Rex turned now to watch big Tom Wilks stride across the frozen brown moss of the pasture. Terran cattle, Rex had learned, thrived on the prickly stuff.

Tom Wilks had a big, cordial face, roughened and seamed by the Martian cold. He slapped Rex on the shoulder and said, "Well, how do you like this outpost of civilization?"

"It's different—I'll say that."

"Hope you grow to like it. A man can get rich out here."

"I don't doubt it."

"You aren't like the others," Wilks said.

"Thank you."

"I mean most of the help we get out here are drifters looking for a stake. You could easy get yourself some land—make a go of it. We need good solid men out here. Now I've got a fine looking daughter—" Wilks paused. "Guess maybe I'm going too fast."

"Jean's a fine girl, but you don't know much about me, Mr. Wilks."

"The name's Tom and don't forget it. And don't think I'm going to nose into your business until you're ready to tell us. We're inclined to take people at face value. We consider 'em first-rate until they prove otherwise. You might say we kind of follow our instincts."

Rex gave him a quick smile. "One thing puzzles me."

"What's that?"

"How come there are no Martians working for you? The pay is good. I'd think they'd be swarming around."

"You don't know much about Mars, son. I've got a hunch there aren't many Martians."

When Rex started to reply, Tom Wilks waved a hand. "Oh, I know the Federation experts tell us different— say they live up there under the ice cap, but I don't believe it. A few of them would wander down."

"Young Tommy tells me you've got one around. A character named Barzoo."

"Uh-huh. God knows where he came from or what he wants here. Doesn't care to work a lick."

This, Rex realized, was Tom Wilks' basis of judging a man. A worker rated high with him. A fairly presentable worker rated high enough to be considered for his daughter's hand. Not a bad way to look at it at that, Rex thought.

"I'd like to meet this Barzoo."

"Tommy'll take you out there any time you say."

"He goes alone?"

"The old coot's harmless. Looked him over myself. He takes the youngster fishing."

"Characters like that interest me."

"Well, finish this fence now and then get back to the house. Jean's fixed up something a little special for supper. Got her hair and face all shined up too. I wonder why?"

Wilks winked and strode off about his business, leaving Rex to wonder about Jean. He'd have to be a little careful there. She was a nice kid. There'd be no problem, though, because he wouldn't be around long enough. He hooked the last strand of wire into place and headed for the house...

JEAN Wilks was a lithe, slim, dark-haired girl with laughing blue eyes and red, almost sensuous lips. When

Rex got to the house she was there to open the door. She wore a close-fitting blouse, slacks, and a frilly postage stamp apron. There was welcome in her smile and her eyes spoke quite frankly. They said, *I'm after you.*

"Come on in and shuck your coat," Jean said. "I'll bet you're frozen."

"Only my fingers."

Jean took his hand in hers and rubbed briskly. Her eyes teased. "I thought you were too hot-blooded to let a little cold snap chill you."

"I'm used to a hot sun."

She could change mood quickly. Her smile slipped away. "Where *did* you come from, Rex?"

As he hesitated she put a quick finger over his lips. "Don't tell me. Sorry I pried. We aren't that way here on Mars—really." She moved away from him. "How do you like my apron! It's supposed to show you how domestic I am."

"You did the cooking tonight?"

"Uh-huh. Mom and Dad and Tommy just left. They went to New Iowa for dinner with some friends. I'm in charge of the feed bag."

"Swell—let's open it up."

Supper over, Rex helped Jean with the dishes. He was struck by the domestic situation into which this case had brought him. He felt guilty—as though he was trespassing on the hospitality of these fine people. And fine people they were—of that he was assured. Now only remained to discover by what weird turn of circumstances the perfectly preserved body of Professor Spencer had been placed in a sealed potato hold in New Iowa.

"The ships that go out of here," Rex said. "Do they all set down in New Iowa—on the field there?"

They were having coffee in the living room. Jean had removed her apron and sat close to Rex on the lounge. Her hair was soft and gleaming in the light of the open flame from the old-fashioned fireplace.

"Usually," she said. "except during heavy harvest time. Then they put down wherever they can. We've had them parked in our lower pasture. You see we like to get the crops away as quick as we can and the freight company always sends enough ships to accommodate use because the run is so profitable."

"The lower pasture. Isn't that where this Barzoo fellow hangs out?"

Jean shuddered. "He's awful. I suppose I shouldn't feel this way about him because he's harmless and very good to Tommy. But that dull-brown hide—his funny eyes."

"I'd like to see what he looks like. I'll have to ask Tommy to take me down there."

Jean regarded him thoughtfully. "I'll take you down."

"But why should you—?"

She shrugged. "I don't seem to be doing very well by firelight. We have two moons up here. They should be twice as hard to resist as one."

Rex was playing it straight all the way through—which meant playing it dumb. "But it's very cold out."

"Pretty cold in here, too. Let's get started."

REX put on his jacket, wondering what he was going to do with this girl. She appeared from her bedroom a few moments later wearing a white parka that made her look doubly attractive. "It's only about a ten-minute walk. And the cold isn't as penetrating here as on Terra."

They hiked along, hand-in-hand, under the two racing Martian moons. The air was sharp, stinging, like heady wine. Rex felt as though he could have jumped clear up to where Terra hung close and beautiful in the night sky. This, he decided, was a wonderful planet, a wonderful country, a great place to settle down and build something—raise children. Bodies in shipping cases seemed far away and unreal.

Jean's hand, warm in his own, squeezed suddenly as though she sensed his thoughts. She glanced at him, her eyes rich with meaning. Then she broke away and ran on ahead toward an oddly shaped monolith of a hut further down the pasture.

As Rex hurried forward, he studied the stone hutch. It was obviously very old—probably something left over from some lost and forgotten civilization. It impressed him as having been built with two purposes—as both a shelter and a symbol. There appeared to be undecipherable meaning in the formation of it—blurred now by the wear of centuries.

Jean stopped beside the narrow entrance. "He's not here," she said. Rex pushed his head inside, bent forward to peer about the small interior. It was smooth, unadorned cone-shaped.

He took a step forward, heard a quick female laugh, and tripped over Jean's extended foot. He grabbed as he tottered and went down—inside the shelter—and caught Jean's arm. He dragged her with him and they went down in a heap. He was looking into her fur-framed face, into her beautiful eyes. She had stopped laughing altogether. Neither of them spoke during several quick breaths.

Then Jean said, "I guess you think I'm pretty forward, don't you?"

"I think you're pretty wonderful."

"I think maybe we're different up here—a lot different than we'd be on Terra."

Her breath was warm in Rex's face. "How do you figure that?"

"We're more elemental out here, I guess. We're more afraid of letting life get past us. I'm not afraid to look you in the eyes and tell you that I want you so bad it hurts. I want to marry you and have your children and I'm afraid of not letting you know it."

Her mouth was on his; her body through the soft fur of their clothing was warm and rounded against him. His blood was pounding and he was conscious of two things. First, this intoxicating girl in his arms. Second, the fact that the slab against which he was pressed had loosened and turned; that it had moved on a hinge of some kind and he had to hold tight to Jean to keep from falling through.

Then he became aware of a third presence. Just outside a figure loomed; a hideous looking man with a brown, scarred hide. A man with eyes that seemed to hold all the hate in the universe...

* * *

(From the Diary of Tommy Wilks) (Saturday)

They're gone—my sister Jean and that Rex Tate fellow. Nobody around here knows what to think because there is no place to go. No ships have come in or gone out. Everybody is talking about it. Some people say Rex Tate had a ship and that he put Jean in it and took her somewhere far away. But how can that be true? Where could anybody hide a ship around here? The country is flat as far as you can see. They say he must have had a ship hidden up in the ice country—in the forbidden circle and he took her up there.

But that is crazy too. They were having supper here last night when Mom and Dad and I went to the Parker's for supper. They weren't here when we got back and none of the cars or horses are gone so how could they have got away?

They say he took Jean away, but I wonder if it really wasn't the other way around? I know that Jean was in love with him—she wanted to marry him—and I wonder if maybe she didn't take HIM away? But that's foolish, too. There was no place for her to take him or him to take her. It certainly is a big mystery. We haven't had so much excitement since we first came to Mars. People coming and going—men riding off in bunches hunting under every piece of moss as though they'd turned to midgets and were hiding there. It all seems very silly to me. But Mom is sick about it. She's in bed and Mrs. Parker has been over a lot taking care of her. The men swear they'll catch Rex and kill him wherever they find him. They say he dragged Jean away to have her for himself, I don't think so—not for that reason, anyhow. I know how Jean felt about him and girls in love are funny. He wouldn't have had to drag her anywhere. That was how Jean felt about him.

It's all very strange. And very lonesome here with Dad gone off with the hunting party and Mom under sedatives. I'm going to ask Barzoo what he thinks about it.

* * *

(Sunday)

I've learned something important and I don't know what to do about it. I went to Barzoo's hutch to find him but he was not there. I waited around a while and then, while I was looking inside, I thought I saw something funny about the wall. One section of it looked different than the others. It wasn't dirty along the bottom. It looked as though there was a crack there. I examined it and found it moved on a hinge. I pushed it back and everything was dark behind it. I listened for a while and then thought I heard a sound inside as though somebody had taken a step.

I got scared and dropped the stone back into place and began to run. I ran all the way home to tell Dad about it because that must be where Rex and Jean went. There can't be any other place.

But Dad isn't here and I can't tell Mom. She's too sick and I'd only disturb her.

It's been an hour now. Dad still isn't home. I've done some thinking. Why did I run away from the hutch? There isn't anything there to be afraid of. When you think it over, it's logical that Barzoo would have a place underneath the hutch to keep warm on cold winter nights. Even if his hide is thick, he still needs shelter. And why should he have told me about it? It's his private business and I never asked him. I'll bet he would have told me if I'd asked him.

I'm going to wait another half-hour for Dad. Then, if he isn't back, I'll go to the hutch with a flashlight and see what's under it. Maybe everybody is right about Rex. Maybe he's got Jean down there.

But if he has I'll bet she isn't trying very hard to get away ...

The half-hour's up. Here I go...

CHAPTER THREE

"SO that's the story," Rex said. "Now you know who I am and how I happened to come to New Iowa."

Jean twisted her arms against the thongs that bound her wrists and said, "I think you were stupid not to tell us and let us try to help you."

"But I was moving in the dark entirely unsure of myself. I had to look around and find out—"

"Oh, I see. You suspected us. You thought we were capable of murdering a man and putting his body in a box and shipping it back to Terra with our potatoes!"

"I thought no such thing!"

They spoke openly, convinced that the five Martians who were their captors could not understand Terran. They had been at the hutch when Rex and Jean got there—four of them—crouched behind the wall. When Barzoo arrived, just as Rex tilted the section of wall, they had seized the two Terrans and tied their hands. There had been nothing Rex could do, hampered as he was by Jean lying in his arms.

Rex's thoughts had been the bitterest of gall as he forecast his report to The Chief—that was, if he lived long enough to submit a report:

I was necking with a local farmer's daughter in the stone hutch of a Martian character. I had every reason to be suspicious of this Martian and should have been on my toes when he arrived. Instead, I was on my back, kissing this aforementioned local daughter and this Martian and four of his friends took us both. No credit to them, though. In the shape we were in, a crippled blind man could have taken us. Any further orders, Chief?

The Martians had ignored his pleas that they leave Jean behind, or perhaps the Martians did not even understand him.

They had been led off down a long, dark tunnel. So far as Rex and Jean were concerned, their next step could have almost dropped them off into oblivion but the Martians were sure-footed and seemed to be entirely familiar with the pitch-black tunnel.

They walked for what seemed hours before a light showed in the distance. Another hour brought them to the spot where a dusty overhead bulb glowed dimly. It appeared to have been there untouched for centuries because the ceiling was damp and calcium-bearing droplets had almost covered it. Yet it glowed bravely.

Here, the two Terrans were allowed to rest. One of the Martians dug into a small opening in one wall and brought forth a quantity of grayish substance that he offered them—holding it toward their mouths with his filthy hand. They turned their faces away and he made no further effort to feed them.

They were ignored—left sitting on a ledge while the Martians gorged down the food. Afterward, the one Jean designated as Barzoo, looked up suddenly as though a thought had come. He talked to one who had finished eating and was wiping his hands on his dull brown hide.

Rex tried to fathom Barzoo's words. Familiar with languages and dialects the System over, he got some of Barzoo's meaning. The Martian leader was worried about the condition in which the hutch floor had been left. Perhaps the wall-section had been left tilted. After a while, the other Martian got to his feet and trotted back through the darkness along the tunnel through which they had come.

AFTER the Martian left, Barzoo wiped his mouth with the back of his hand and motioned Rex and Jean to get up and move into a passage to their right.

"How much further can he take us?" Jean asked. "After the first drop back at the hutch, it seems to me the tunnel has been level."

"A floor can be deceptive. We could have been moving down a gradual slope for miles."

Jean said nothing. The going was easier now, this tunnel being lighted at intervals by the strange overhead bulbs. Rex asked, "Are you sore at me for what happened back at the farm? For not telling you the truth?"

"No. We're in too much trouble to waste time being angry. What's done is done. Only the future is important now."

Rex could have made his self-recrimination vocal but he felt that too would be a waste of time. He said, "Didn't anybody—any of you Terrans know about the opening in that hutch?"

"I'm sure no one did—except perhaps Tommy." She thought that over and added, "No—that's absurd. If Tommy had known it he wouldn't have been able to keep it to himself."

"Maybe they'll hunt around and find it."

"Maybe—but I hope they don't."

"Why not?"

"If they find the opening they'll come looking for us. These Martians are hostile. Some of our men might be killed and they have wives and families."

Jean made Rex feel ashamed of himself. "Don't worry. I'll get you out of here."

She glanced up at him. Her chin trembled slightly as she sought to stiffen it.

At that moment they walked into a larger tunnel. There were more overhead bulbs here and a ribbon of narrow-gauge track stretching off into the distance.

"A railroad!" Rex exclaimed.

"I wonder where it goes?"

"I've got a hunch we're going to find out."

One of the Martians had gone around a shoulder of the tunnel. There was a whining sound. He returned in the driver's seat of a small rail car. Barzoo motioned the Terrans into one of the seats. The other Martians got in behind them. The driver pulled a throttle. The whining sound increased and the car moved off down the tracks.

Rex listened for a time, inspected the portion of the car within range of his eyes, then said, "I wonder what kind of power this thing uses?"

Jean did not answer. Her head had dropped to his shoulder. She was asleep. He settled himself, forming a pocket with his body so she could rest against him with the seat supporting her. Behind him the eyes of the three Martians, including Barzoo, had also closed. Rex wondered if the driver was asleep also.

The car rolled on in a monotonously straight line, mile after mile. Rex realized he had discovered a civilization under Mars, the existence of which was unknown on Terra. He knew that none of the authorities or experts suspected anything so civilized as a railroad in the forbidden polar lands. At best they thought the territory inhabited by hardy bands of hostile, backward ice dwellers.

This was indeed a great discovery he told himself bitterly. Of course neither he nor Jean would live to reveal it, but they could die happy, knowing they were great explorers.

He grew tired of excoriating himself. The passing overhead lights had a hypnotic effect. He closed his eyes and slept.

FANTON, son of Fandor of the Bantarks—last great ruling dynasty of Mars—lay sick and dying in a foul cell under the Amphitheater of the Gods. He was old and tired and ready to die, yet he longed for survival because his work was not yet done.

For two centuries, Fanton had ruled as Lord of the North Hemisphere. He had seen the great prosperity of the planet even under conditions whereby the scientists of his father had foreseen the planet's death. He had been there at the birth of their scientific magic.

Fandor, his father, had been a wise and gentle ruler. When the Terrans came in their great ships, Fandor had prevailed upon the Council and a policy of cautious retreat had been instituted. Fandor advocated this because he knew the Martian science was no match for that of the Terrans. Not that the wizardry of the Martian scientists was any less great, but they had bent their efforts in peaceful directions while the Terrans came with huge warships and no end of armament.

So the Martians, under Fandor, had retreated quietly to the north allowing the Terrans to move onto the planet. This policy was much despised by the young and the hotheaded who would have preferred to meet the invader face to face and die in battle if need be. But the majority of the Council was old and weary as was Fandor, and they prevailed.

Then Fandor felt he had lived long enough and refused to enter the place of Eternal Strength—greatest miracle of Martian science. He died peacefully and Fanton put on his royal robes.

Now those robes had been torn from his body and he had been refused access to the place of Eternal Strength. Pandek, the fiery young Councilman had overthrown him and assumed power, and the younger Martians were preparing to sweep down over the planet and slay the unsuspecting Terrans.

They would be slaughtered of course. This, Fanton knew, because the Martian weapons were puny, but there would be death and fiery agony before the Terrans finally won.

Many times, in his heart, Fanton had wondered if the policy of the old ones had been wise. Fanton was a scholar. The books of the Terrans had been smuggled into the north country. He had learned the language and read the books and there was one Terran writer of whom he never tired; a genius named William Shakespeare. In his great play called *Julius Caesar,* Shakespeare had said: *There is a tide in the affairs of men which taken at its flood leads on to fortune.*

Lying in his filthy cell, Fanton's mind was cloudy. He was not sure if those were the exact words but the point was clear. Perhaps there had been a time in the affairs of the Martians when the tide of fortune was at its flood— when they could have won out over the Terrans. But that time had certainly long-passed and if their present plight was the result of the old mistakes, then so be it. There was still no justification for mass suicide.

So Fanton did not want to die. His work remained undone. Above his cell, in the Amphitheater of the Gods, Pantek was fomenting a kettle of hell's brew. Already, they had used the Place of Eternal Strength in a fiendish manner—desecrated it—and now they deprived their Emperor of its healing magic.

Fanton realized the die was cast. He himself had been removed from the stage. Mad new actors bent upon destruction were reading their lines.

He, Fanton, was finished...

TOMMY Wilks walked a long way down the dark passage, his light picking a path through the gloom. He knew he had already gone further than he should but always there was the temptation to see what lay just ahead.

And nothing was ever there. Only the sinister black passage leading onward. He explored another length, then stopped. This was far enough. What if he had unknowingly turned into a by-passage? Suppose he would miss the intersection on the way back?

Thoughts such as these flared into his mind to bring a sudden license of entrapment. The walls seemed to be closing in on him. He turned to retrace his steps.

Then he froze. Sound. A far away, echoing sound. The soft tap of footsteps. But coming closer. Tommy threw his light on down the tunnel. He strained his eyes ahead looking for whatever or whoever made the sound.

It was louder now and he realized, too late, that his flash was on—guiding the menace—serving as a beacon. He clawed at the switch but his fingers were clumsy thumbs. When he finally got the light out, the footsteps had increased to a running tempo. He turned and fled blindly back along the tunnel. He had not taken ten steps when he tripped and fell. He struggled to his feet in panic. Too late. Hard, rough hands were upon him.

He fought but his struggles were useless.

CHAPTER FOUR

TWICE, Rex had tried to maneuver the Martians into removing the thongs from his wrists. At the end of the rail line there was a pool of water fed by a spring. He motioned toward his wrists and signified thirst. One of the Martians callously threw water in his face until he was gasping for breath. His second attempt failed also and now he and Jean were being led through a shining marble corridor the like of which he had never seen even in the finer buildings on Terra. What manner of world, he wondered, was hidden here under the northern Martian ice cap?

But the wonder in store made the corridor look like a tunnel clawed through bare earth. It was a huge amphitheater into which he and Jean were rudely shoved. They stood frozen, their perilous position momentarily forgotten.

"Did you ever see anything like it?" Jean gasped.

"It must be an illusion of some kind. I can't believe it really exists."

The floor upon which they stood was of pure, glittering gold. It stretched away in shining glory to a wall of crystal—a window so high and vast Rex could not conceive it as standing alone. Surely it had to fall by its own weight.

It dwarfed a high, curved dais along which sat a line of richly robed Martians. In the center of the dais was an elevated throne upon which sat a scowling young Martian.

But the thing that caught and held the two Terrans were the towering cliffs of ice framed in the great window as by a master painter. Rex and Jean were pushed forward. As they came near the high throne, the young Martian smiled coldly as he noted the direction of their eyes.

He broke the silence. "You seem to admire our view."

"You speak Terran." Rex said, surprise in his words.

"A source of amazement to you, no doubt. You who consider us a mob of imbeciles cringing up here in the ice floes."

"Whoever you are, I'm afraid you're in serious trouble. We aren't used to being hauled around like criminals."

"Then it's time you got used to it."

"Who are you?"

"I am Pandek, ruler of all Martians. Down on your knees!"

Rex and Jean were hurled roughly to the floor. Rex lowered his head and whispered to Jean, "Take it easy. We've got to feel our way and wait this out." To Pandek, he said, "Is this the way you're in the habit of receiving ambassadors from friendly nations?"

"Friendly? That from you who have kicked and despised us for hundreds of years?" Pandek's rage was heightening with each word he spoke. "You and your arrogant army of Terran invaders? You who treated us with the patronizing kindness you reserve for amiable dogs?"

"We came in friendship—"

"—with armed spaceships at your back—uninvited—unwelcome—smiling like the hypocrites you are…"

"Those entrusted with government on Terra would be happy to hear that you are willing to come forth and negotiate," Rex said.

Pandek arose from his throne, his brown face mottled with rage. "Negotiate for what is already ours? Put our stamp of approval on your conquest of our planet?"

Rex saw that further words were useless. He stood silent until the ruler's anger subsided. Then he asked, "What do you plan to do with us?"

"Kill you—as we will kill every Terran on our world."

HE eyed Rex for signs of fear. When they did not appear he seemed mildly disappointed. When he spoke again it was in a quieter tone. "But first I would have you see a little of what Martian science is like. I would have you know how far ahead of the Terran bunglers our scientists were even a thousand years ago. I would have you know by what power Mars will again come into its own."

"I would like to see the work of your scientists." Conceit was obviously one of this ruler's weaknesses, Rex decided. He hoped others would reveal themselves.

"Very well, Terran. You shall see a part of the miracle concerning which you Terrans have wondered for years; the miracle by which your stolen lands below the polar circle have been watered and kept lush."

"The ice cliffs?"

"Yes. I cannot show you the process whereby the rains and the snows are created and drawn to the pole each season—how these great cliffs of ice are built over the winter months. But I can reveal to you the most spectacular part of the process—the melting of the ice cliffs."

In spite of their predicament, Rex was vitally interested. Jean, also. He glanced at her and saw the intent look on her face.

Pandek picked up a device at his elbow—obviously some sort of a telephone and spoke into it. His words were low and undistinguishable. But the results were almost instantaneous.

A far-away hum was heard, greatening in volume as from the release of sudden power. A faint blue light appeared, causing the ice to glow at the base of the cliffs. The color shot up through the ice mass—clear blue—as new colors were added to that at the base. Red, yellow, purple, crimson—so bright they seemed to sear Rex's eyes. Then they too started climbing up through the solid ice.

A deep, ominous rumbling was heard. Pandek said, "Your Terran scientists have not even begun to fully realize the incalculable power of nuclear fission. Two thousand years ago our scientists were ages ahead of them."

Pandek said more, but his words were completely drowned in the thunder from the crashing of ice cliffs beyond the great window. Huge cataracts were even now pouring down the walls of melting ice. Both Rex and Jean stood awed at the sight of such vast and instantaneous destruction.

Pandek smiled his cold smile. The thunder subsided somewhat and Pandek said, "I see you are impressed. I would welcome your comments." He was enjoying himself.

The display had astounded Rex but the expression on his face remained cold. "I imagine you were responsible for sending the body of Professor Spencer back to Terra."

PANDEK paused at Rex's quick change of subject. "Yes, a fitting reminder to the Terrans that we aren't animals to be gaped at."

"On the contrary—an indication that you *are* animals."

Pandek half-rose from the throne. "You'll die a little more horribly than I'd planned for that remark."

"Perhaps I will, but the fact remains that you're mad to think you can stand against Terra. Your scientific know-how is admittedly great, but it is not geared for war."

"You think not?"

"I'm certain of it. I'm also sure of another thing."

"What else are you sure of?"

"That you have no scientists."

"Then how—?"

"You had them—ages ago—and they built well—so well that their work has survived to this very day. What you have here was built by geniuses for fools to operate. I'm certain all you do is press switches and reap the benefits of work done by long-dead brains in another age."

The darkening of Pandek's face told Rex his words had cut deep. In a way, he felt sorry for the Martian. A hate-filled, envy-charged man seeking to vent his rage in mad ways.

If carried to their ultimate, his acts could only lead to the destruction of his people at the hands of the Terrans. But this made the situation no less perilous for Rex and Jean and other Terrans on Mars.

"You hold a Terran citizen," he said. The daughter of Professor Spencer. Is she still alive?"

Pandek was again enjoying himself. "Oh, very much so." His smile held some hidden meaning as he said, "A trifle embarrassed perhaps—at the moment—but alive and healthy."

"I demand you return her to her own people."

"You demand? I admire your courage."

"What do you plan to do with her?"

Pandek's Martian eyes grew speculative. "I will need her. She fits into my plans as does the young woman at your side. There is a new day is coming. It will dawn upon Mars soon, a reversion to the old days when Mars was a virile, fighting planet. Back then, there was far less science and much more emotion. The masses were whipped to a fighting frenzy by supplications to the old gods." Pandek grinned a malevolent smile. "Human sacrifices were a part of those supplications. Nothing stirs the people like the public sacrifice of a beautiful female with all its pomp and splendor. It stirs them deeply."

"The thought of it stirs *you* deeply. Isn't that what you really mean? You're mad. You're a dangerous maniac. I can only hope your own people put you down in time."

With a howl of rage, Pandek leaped from his throne. He drew a short ornamental sword from his belt and swung it viciously against the side of Rex's head. Rex went down like an ox felled for slaughter.

Jean screamed…

CHAPTER FIVE

THE rough-skinned Martian who subdued Tommy Wilks, pressed him against the wall of the tunnel and used Tommy's own flashlight for purposes of inspection. He growled a few unintelligible words and seemed to be debating a problem.

Tommy watched him silently, warily, without fear. He had ceased struggling because it was useless, but his mind was alert.

He had no way of knowing the Martian was in a quandary. He had been sent to check the tunnel entrance in the stone hutch on the Wilks farm. But he had come upon Tommy halfway to his objective. Should he take Tommy to his superiors, or finish his original mission? It was indeed a problem.

The Martian was not too bright. Also, he was lazy. The capturing of this Terran changed things, he told himself. He would take the boy to the terminal. Then perhaps something would happen so he would not have to take the long walk back through the tunnel. Perhaps he would be honored for his capture and another would be sent to the hutch.

This hope brightened him as he took Tommy roughly by the arm and hauled him toward the railhead. Tommy was not a difficult prisoner. They moved swiftly. But the boy was breathing heavily when he was pushed into one of the cars and the Martian took the controls.

Tommy rested, awaiting his chance. He had by no means given up hope. It was just a matter of the Martian easing up on his arm. At least that would be the first step. Tommy was glad the Martian had been contemptuous and not tied him up.

The car rolled smoothly along its tracks; faster than the one used to transport Rex and Jean because the Martian transporting Tommy had always liked speed. He liked it so well he opened the car to its greatest capacity and at one point had to release Tommy's arm in order to put both hands on the throttle.

Tommy struck instantly without thought as to the outcome—only with hope. And his hopes were fulfilled. He hurled himself against the Martian with both fists extended. They hit hard brown hide just below the Martian's right shoulder and sent him off balance. The Martian snatched at Tommy while trying to regain his equilibrium and learned the folly of attempting two things at once.

But too late. He teetered, howled dismally, and pitched in front of the racing car. It hit him with a dull thud, killing him instantly. But his dead bulk also wreaked a kind of vengeance on the car, lifting it from its tracks and sending it skidding along on its side.

Tommy had been thrown clear and as he hit the wall of the tunnel he knew he was done for. Every bone in his body snapped. Every ounce of his flesh crackled with pain. He fell to the tracks and lay dying.

But the process was slower than he anticipated. A full minute passed and he had not yet expired. This puzzled him. How could you live with all this pain? With every bone broken? It just didn't make sense. Tommy waited.

But death proved remarkably stubborn. It refused to drop its black mantle over his tortured body. Finally Tommy moved an arm—a foot—a leg. Odd. They all worked. He got to his feet. He conceded that maybe the agony was not as great as it had first seemed. Now that he could breath again, things were better. There was only one bad place, really; a vicious bloody abrasion along his right forearm.

The lights of a platform loomed ahead. Tommy crawled over the car and stepped gingerly around the body of the dead Martian. Then he hurried forward and climbed on the deserted platform.

Here the light was better and he examined his arm. It was an angry, bloody mass but the blood was oozing out rather than flowing. No deep wound had been suffered but it hurt like fury. He could not bear to have anything touch it so he put his arm out at an awkward angle and left it there while he looked around, wondering what this place was and also how hard you had to get hit and how much it had to hurt before you got killed.

HIS ponderings were interrupted by the sound of footsteps. In the face of this, there was nothing to do, he decided, but pick a direction and run. Back up the tracks? No. While the lights from the overhead bulbs were dim, they would still reveal him at quite a distance. The platform had two exits. The running footsteps were approaching along one of these. That left the other. Tommy plunged into it and ran.

He ran a long way and his surroundings changed swiftly. The rail platform had been crude and uninspiring but now he was fleeing along a beautiful marble corridor.

He stopped for breath, backed into a partially secluded niche and admired his surroundings. Was this the kind of place the Martians lived in? It certainly didn't fit into his preconceived notions of a place where backward ice people would dwell.

As his breathing lessened, a tantalizing sound asserted itself upon his ears. An odd, singing sound, both pleasant and mysterious. He wondered where it came from.

He peeked out into the corridor and found it deserted.

The singing sound. As he walked back along the corridor, it diminished. He turned and retraced his steps. The sound greatened until he came to an archway in one wall of the corridor. The sound obviously emanated from that direction. The archway was supported by gleaming marble pillars and as Tommy passed between them, the singing sound rose to a crescendo that vibrated deliciously against his nerve centers.

Then he saw it. A beautiful, domed room that gave a first impression of being a public bath of some sort. But there was no water, only brilliant, breathtaking color; all the gorgeous colors of the rainbow dancing down from the ceiling in beams of crystal clarity. There was sound and color—and something else; a subtle something that made Tommy very happy; excitedly happy in a way he had never before experienced.

He moved forward, completely engrossed in his new surroundings. He moved in under the shower of color and a feeling of ecstatic exhilaration went through him. It was wonderful.

Then he froze. Not twenty feet away stood two Martians clad in rich metal harness and holding long golden spears. Guards. Sudden fear swept Tommy. The Martians were staring straight at him.

Desperately, he signaled to his frozen muscles; *Let's get out of here.* But they failed to respond. The guards stared at him. He stared back.

Nothing happened.

Why, they're asleep, Tommy thought in amazement. They're standing there sound asleep with their eyes wide open holding their spears. That's crazy. Why don't they fall down?

Tommy wanted to run. But he couldn't. The curiosity of the very young not only barred retreat, but pushed him slowly forward until he was standing beside one of the guards.

The Martian had not moved a muscle. His chest neither rose nor fell. Completely fascinated, Tommy extended his hand. He touched the face of the guard. It was rough and cool. The guard did not move, Tommy laid a hand against the golden harness. Nothing happened. He had not intended to push, but he did. He pushed so hard the guard tilted over on one stiff leg. Appalled, Tommy leaped back.

The guard kept on tilting until he fell on his side with a great crash of ringing metal.

TOMMY darted back through the color rays and out of the strange room so fast that he was far down the marble hall before his mind told him he was running.

He kept on running. Then he stopped as suddenly as he had started. He looked down at his wounded arm. He glanced quickly up and down the corridor, then ducked again in a wall niche where he gave his whole attention to his arm.

Had he dreamed all this? The horrible Martian in the tunnel? The car crash? The color room? He must have dreamed it. The proof was there before him. A smooth, unblemished forearm where there had been a huge bloody bruise but a few moments before! He rubbed the arm—tested it. There was not the faintest sign of a wound.

He looked around in bewilderment, peeked both ways and moved out again into the corridor.

His luck had held for a long time but now it failed him as sudden footsteps sounded in a traversing passage just ahead. They were coming swiftly. Tommy looked around in desperation.

This appeared to be the end but it was not. Fate seemed indeed to be toying with him—moving him around like a mobile chessman. At the last moment it showed him a doorway he had overlooked. The door was unlocked and he went through it as fast as he could while still closing it softly behind him.

Inside, the light was very dim. Tommy listened at the door as the sound of footsteps diminished. He smiled— quite proud of his ability to take care of himself under these circumstances. He would certainly have a lot to put in his diary when he got home.

If he got home.

Tommy drove this last thought from his mind. He would make it. He was doing all right. Whereupon fate slapped him, and sharply, for his conceit by turning him and dropping him down a flight of stairs—he'd been too busy watching the door to notice.

The fall hurt but Tommy was no longer frightened. He knew that so long as he had survived the car crash no violence of this type could even dent him.

He got to his feet and danced around for a while, holding a barked shin, then straightened as a new sound smote his ears. Someone was sobbing.

A woman. A woman crying.

It did not take Tommy long to trace the sound. He was in a narrower, lower corridor now; one not as fine as the big one upstairs. As Tommy moved forward, the sobbing told him he was going in the right direction. He opened a door.

Inside the small room was a narrow, high-legged bed—more of a table, Tommy thought, but he gave it no attention. He was held spellbound by what lay upon the table.

A girl with wrists and ankles bound down. She had long chestnut hair that hung down over the edge of the table. She was helpless. And she was completely nude…

CHAPTER SIX

REX got up from the floor to which he had been viciously hurled by three Martian guards. He and Jean were in a cell. As the barred door danged shut, he turned to help Jean as best he could. "Are you hurt?"

"I—I guess not." She tried to smile. Only my dignity."

"I got us into a pretty bad mess."

"It wasn't your fault."

"I don't know who's else it was."

Jean strained at her bonds. "They could have at least taken these things off our wrists."

"We can do it ourselves."

"That guard out there—he's leering in. Maybe we'd better wait until he leaves."

"Maybe he won't leave. Anyhow—I don't think they care whether we take them off or not."

They stood back to back while Rex worked on the thongs binding Jean. The knots were stubborn but they finally gave, the guard outside watching the process with amusement.

Jean got Rex's wrist free quickly and they sat down on the edge of the single bunk and rubbed their wrists. "Well," Jean said, "where do we go from here?"

"To wherever they execute their prisoners, I imagine."

"But we're still alive. Aren't we supposed to keep the chin up like they do in books?"

He took her suddenly in his arms. "You're a brave girl."

She pressed close to him. "I'd rather hear you say I'm an attractive girl."

He kissed her hard. "Does that convince you?"

She sighed and snuggled closer, oblivious of the leering guard. "Thanks, mister. That's better. A gal doesn't mind dying, but she hates to go out feeling she hasn't hooked her man."

Rex felt a catch in his throat at the brave front she was maintaining. And it had to be an effort. Jean was no fool. She was a realist. No need to tell her they were finished—that he was no superman who could kick down a wall and carry her to safety.

"Let's not think about anything but us," she whispered. "We have at least a few minutes to live. Really live…"

"With that guard standing there?" Rex said bitterly.

"Well, then we can almost live." She kissed him.

A few minutes later, he said, "Did you notice anything funny out there in that council room?"

"What do you mean by funny? I was so busy looking at those tumbling ice cliffs—"

"I mean the councilmen sitting on either side of Pandek. Not one of them moved or spoke."

"That's right. They sat there like dummies."

"A row of dummies afraid to move even their eyes."

"There's something else that puzzles me," Jean said. "Those ice cliffs are life and death to we Terrans down below. Then why do the Martians build them up each winter and melt them for us in the spring? I'd think they'd leave the plains arid and thus drive us out."

"I wondered about that too. There can be only one explanation. They've repeated the process for so long they're afraid to stop—afraid of what it might do to the overall welfare of the planet."

"Perhaps if they didn't the ice would pile up of its own accord and crush them and their cities."

"I wonder how many cities there are."

"I don't care—really. Hold me closer. I'm cold…"

"BUT I don't understand why they would do such a thing as this," Tommy said. He had released the girl and found her clothing in a corner of the room.

"It is a part of some pagan rite they plan to revive. The victim must lie in—in the manner you found me for a certain length of time. Some weird looking priests visited me at intervals and recited incantations. It was horrible!"

"What's your name?"

"My name's Helen Spencer. I came here with my father…"

"Never mind that now. I think we can get out of here. There was nobody in the hallway when I came in."

"I'd like to find my father."

"We can try."

"They separated us a long time ago. For a while they treated me like a queen, even though they kept me a prisoner. I wondered why. Now I know. It was all a part of this terrible pagan sacrifice. I think the time is very near."

"Then let's go."

But they had waited too long. The door opened and four Martian guards entered. They almost filled the room. Tommy hurled himself at the closest one but was knocked viciously back against the wall. It seemed that fate had deserted him at last.

The Martian in charge, one who stood a head taller than the other three, grasped Helen roughly by the arm. He seemed infuriated at finding her dressed. He threw her roughly after Tommy and she too fell to the floor.

The Martian stood there, undecided, some problem evidently occupying his mind. The three subordinates waited in silence. After a few moments, the leader turned and barked several sharp commands.

The orders puzzled the three Martians. They stood where they were until the leader barked another sharper order. Then they turned and filed out.

The leader stood motionless until their footsteps died in the corridor. Then he bent swiftly and lifted Helen Spencer to her feet.

As she cringed away, he said, "I am Maxis, a doctor in the Emperor's guard. I think perhaps you can help me. If so, I may be able to help you."

"You—you're speaking Terran," Helen said.

"Of course. Many of us know your language." He pointed to Tommy. "Who is this one?"

"I don't know. But I'm sure he has hurt none of you. Please let him go free."

Maxis shook his head impatiently. "It is of no importance. Tell me—while you lay here bound, did they bring a man to see you? A very old man—very feeble?"

Helen did not trust the Martian. After what had happened to her she was in no mood to trust any of these people. There had been an old man. The priests and a tall young Martian had practically carried him in. They had stayed in the room for quite a while, the young Martian talking harshly. The older one had pleaded with him. Had the old man escaped? Helen wondered. Was this one hunting him down?

"You don't trust me," Maxis said. "but you must. If the old one came he would have been brought by a young one. The old one would have been horrified at seeing you."

"That's how it was," Helen said.

Maxis' eyes flared. He laid a quick hand on Helen's shoulder, then drew it back. "How long ago was this? Tell me! How long ago?"

"Several hours at least."

"Then he still lives. They lied to us. Pandek lied to us."

"If you would explain—"

"The man you saw—the old one—was Fanton, Lord of the North Hemisphere—Ruler of Mars. Pandek told us of his death when he assumed the throne. Only for this reason did the legions swear loyalty to Pandek. But Fanton still lives!"

Tommy had got to his feet and was brushing his clothes. "Maybe not. They might have killed him in the meantime."

"I have a feeling he is not dead," Maxis insisted. "I must find him. I must not fail to find him…"

He was turning toward the door. Tommy said, "What about us?"

Maxis turned back and Tommy knew he was ready to leave them to fend for themselves. Tommy said, "You promised to help us if she told you what you wanted to know."

"You are right. But you will be in my way."

"A promise is a promise," Tommy said stoutly.

"Very well. We will go down to the prison block. You two will march ahead. I will act as though I am delivering you. But if there is any trouble I will have to desert you. I cannot stand and fight. I cannot risk being slain until I find my Emperor."

They marched out into the corridor. The three guards had gone their way and no one was in sight. But from the grim look on the Martian's face, Tommy knew peril lay ahead.

THE door to the cell in which Rex and Jean were imprisoned was unlocked. Five Martian guards entered. The leader was in high rage. "This girl will have to do," he snapped. "The crowds in the square will not know the difference and the priests will just have to keep their mouths shut. Take her..."

As three of the guards advanced on Jean, Rex went into action. He drove his knee into the groin of the leader, bending the Martian forward into a straight right that almost tore his head off. The Martian went down. His jaw structure was so thick, Rex's fist turned numb from the contact and the Martian was only dazed.

Rex knew his one hope lay in getting control of the small pistol the leader carried. He lunged. The gun lay in the fallen leader's outstretched hand. Rex's fingers touched it. But the leader's fist closed.

The delay was fatal. It gave one of the guards time to take one long step and kick Rex solidly behind the right ear. Rex went down hard, smacking the floor with his face. He did not move. Jean screamed. A hard hand went brutally over her mouth, dragging her down also.

The leader of the squad said, "Take her to the ceremonial room. Prepare her for the knife. Tell the priests I will be there soon."

"Aye, great Lord Pandek," the guard said.

Jean bit the hand that lay across her mouth. It was jerked away. She tore loose and threw herself down on Rex's unconscious body. She was pulled roughly to her feet and other hard hands dragged her away.

CHAPTER SEVEN

PERHAPS it was Tommy's luck that carried the party through. On the trip to the cellblocks they met only two other Martians—not soldiers—who exhibited only mild curiosity.

Once in the lower tier, Maxis seemed more at home. "This is the likeliest cell block," he said.

"But we can't search all those cells," Tommy said. "It would take hours. We'd surely be stopped." He was looking down a long corridor lined with bars. Other corridors intersected until the place was a maze.

"You are right," Maxis said. "I have a plan that may save us time. Come. You two walk behind me now."

They moved down the corridor. Only one guard lay in their path but he was down on his haunches, asleep. They glided past him, Maxis' gun held ready. They moved on until they were approaching a more brightly-lighted intersection. A small table was located against the bars of a corner cell and a Martian sat at the table occupied with some papers.

The trio approached from behind the man quietly. He heard them when they were a few steps away. He turned. Maxis took a last bold step and was towering over the seated one.

Maxis spoke casually, but with authority. "I've been sent to deliver Fanton to the council hall."

Maxis did not expect cooperation from the guard. But he hoped for something else. His eyes were on the guard's face, waiting for the man's first reaction.

It was entirely satisfactory from Maxis' point of view. The guard's startled eyes widened, then narrowed in suspicion. "Who sent you for him?"

Maxis smiled without humor. "Then he is here. He does live. What cell, you mother's mistake? Quick!"

The guard looked into the barrel of the deadly gun Maxis held close to his face. A black hole from whence could come needle flames that would burn his head into an instantaneous crisp. "The—third aisle—cell eight—"

The gun in Maxis's hand spit a small blue flame. For a moment, the guard's head was enveloped in fire. Then the head was gone.

Helen Spencer recoiled in horror. Maxis said, "He was a traitor." To the Martian, that justified everything. He bent over and picked up the headless body and carried it into the nearest cell.

He returned and said to Tommy, "This is the dangerous moment. You must help me—do exactly as I say. You must go to the cell and bring Fanton back to this table. I must wait here."

Tommy was perplexed. "I don't get it. You should be better able to get him out of his cell. If we meet a guard, he'll stop us."

"No he won't. He will bring you here. All authority in the block stems from this key-center. If you meet a guard tell him you are under orders from the key-keeper. He will be suspicious and completely confounded, but he will bring you here. In the meantime I can better stave off trouble with the authority this post gives me."

Maxis looked at Helen and pointed. "You—into that cell—out of sight. Stay there until we have either succeeded or failed." His face was grim. "If we fail, you must shift for yourself with nothing but my good wishes to help you on your way."

His tone indicated his good wishes would be of scant aid. He laid a hand on Tommy's shoulder. "Walk to the next intersection down that corridor. Turn to your right and count off seven cells. Fanton will be in the eighth. Good luck."

TOMMY took the key Maxis handed him and started off as directed. The key seemed very heavy. The corridor seemed very long. The task set for him seemed next to impossible.

He reached the cell without trouble. He unlocked the door. Inside, a very old Martian lay in filth and rags on the floor. Tommy knelt beside him, his heart pounding. "You are to come with me," he said.

The old Martian opened his eyes. "Who are you?"

"I am Tommy Wilks, a Terran, but that doesn't matter. Maxis, one of your friends, is waiting at the table down the hall. Can you walk, sir?"

A tired smile brightened the old Martian's face. "Strange indeed are our times—when a Terran juvenile comes to aid the Lord of the North Hemisphere. The times have gone mad and we can only go where destiny directs—or seems to."

Fanton, with Tommy's aid, had got to his feet and Tommy helped him from the cell. But now there was a barrier—three scowling Martian guards. One of them barked a challenge in his own language. "Don't say anything," Tommy warned Fanton. "Maxis said it might work out like this."

To the Martian, he said, "I've been sent to bring the prisoner," but he knew the Martian did not understand him.

The three spoke among themselves, their confusion quite obvious.

Then it worked exactly as Maxis had hoped. At a command from one, the other two guards took Tommy and Fanton each by an arm and hauled them along the corridor toward the key-center. As they approached it, Tommy saw that Maxis had gotten to his feet and was waiting for them. The grim Martian stood with both hands behind his back.

As they came to a halt, the leader of the trio spoke questioningly to Maxis in their own language. Before Maxis could answer, the other's eyes opened wide and Tommy knew what was going on in his mind. He was recognizing Maxis as a false key-keeper.

The leader got short satisfaction from his discovery. He died with his questions still unanswered as Maxis brought his right arm around and blasted the man's head into a cinder.

The other two guards fell away quickly, their reflexes in perfect condition. Both snatched for their own guns, one going down as Maxis' ray cut him in two.

The other guard was bringing his gun up. Maxis had no time to match shots with him or perhaps chose not to from a certainty that both of them would die as a result.

Instead, he hurled himself on the guard and caught the latter's wrist bending the gun away from himself and the others. The guard was far heavier than Maxis, his bulk possessed of greater strength. He dropped the gun but heaved Maxis to one side and come down heavily upon him. He had trapped Maxis' arms successfully and it was a matter of moments before he would again have the gun in his fist.

Tommy acted from desperation—without plan. A heavy ring of keys lay on the desk. Tommy snatched them up and swung them, from high over his head, down hard on the skull of the guard. The guard's head was indeed hard. The keys rang dully against it but the guard's hand only faltered in reaching for the gun.

Tommy swung the keys again and again. Unable to grip the gun, the guard reached with both hands, thus loosing his hold on Maxis for a moment.

The moment was enough. Suddenly the guard stiffened and came awkwardly erect. There was an empty look in his eyes and then Tommy saw the reason. The handle of a dagger protruded from his chest, driven in by Maxis who was even now rolling the corpse over and coming free.

Maxis sheathed his dagger, still dripping blood. He snapped, "We've got to move fast. Now all we have to go on is hope."

Helen came from the cell as Tommy asked, "Where are we going?"

"We've got to get Fanton to the Place of Eternal Strength. Come…" He took the old Martian in his arms and the cavalcade moved off down the corridor following Maxis' lead. Guards could be heard, running in from different directions.

To Maxis, it was but a matter of time. He did not expect to reach the Place of Eternal Strength. He could only try; and die finally, battling for his Emperor. But this did not sadden him. There was no better way for a Martian to die...

REX floated in a sea of pain. Sadistically beaten by the guards who had overpowered him, he lay on the floor of the cell; aware of the blood-pool around him and of the pain, but unable to force his body into action. He knew the door to the cell stood open. He forced his mind to focus on this point. It could mean only one thing.

The guards had left him for dead.

The thought cheered him. He was not dead. Therefore he was living on borrowed time—a break men in his profession seldom got.

Another thought intruded. Maybe he wasn't lucky. Maybe he was crippled. He had as yet not inventoried the damage. Was it worse than the pain indicated?

He searched for numbness and found none. He moved and the pain increased. That was good. Nothing paralyzed. But was an arm or leg broken? Was there a spine injury?

Resolutely, he forced his muscles to respond. Arms, legs, bones okay. He got to his feet and swayed dizzily. Pain shot through his head. For a moment he thought he would black out, but he clawed at the wall and kept himself from falling.

He got hold of a bar and held himself erect while the floor spun and the walls tilted. Then they steadied away. His stomach settled back into place, the nausea giving ground sullenly.

After a while, he decided he was all right. As all right as he would be for a long time. He looked around for a weapon. All the bars were in solid rock. The legs of the bunk were riveted down.

He hunted and stood finally looking at his two fists. They were all he had. They would have to do.

He stepped out of his cell and saw two guards approaching along the corridor. He debated flight. He stopped. There were the two fists. Might as well find out right now how effective they would be. He crouched and stood waiting...

JEAN moved as though she was in a daze. She had been taken by the Martian guard through long corridors, into a splendid part of whatever building this was. At one point during the trip, she lashed out suddenly, bit the hand across her mouth and raked her nails across a hard face.

The Martians had been in no mood to tame a tigress the gentle way. The big Martian, after snarling from the bite, swung his other fist viciously. The blow rang against Jean's head. She fell. The Martians growled at each other, picked her up roughly and carried her, half-conscious, on down the corridor.

She was taken to a high room, far up in the building. The room seemed to be some sort of a storage place for fine garments. They were everywhere; gold surplices hanging in rows; beautiful gold and silver sandals hanging from pegs along the wall. A rich room with windows and daylight coming in; the first Jean had seen in a long time.

She remembered the stone hutch—so wondrous—so far away—so unattainable. Rex. Tears welled in Jean's eyes and she tasted the dregs of bitterness as she saw Rex—in memory—lying bloody and broken on the floor of the cell; recalled the ferocity with which the Martians had attacked him.

Suddenly Jean realized what was going on—what the Martians were doing there in the high room—stripping off her clothing. With a choked cry she found new strength and fought again.

She took them by surprise; broke from them and ran, half-naked, toward the door. Escape seemed imminent—but she threw herself straight into the arms of a tall, scowling Martian who held her like a child and carried her back into the terrible room. As he walked toward them, those who had brought her there fell on their knees. One of them intoned, "Pandek—great Pandek—Lord of the North Hemisphere."

"Not quite," Pandek said, speaking in Terran. "And never if I continue to be surrounded by bungling fools such as you, who cannot hold a slip of a girl. Had I not come through that door she would even now be making her escape."

"She surprised us, great Pandek. It will not happen again."

Callously, Pandek held Jean forth with one great hand and hit her sharply on the point of her chin with a doubled fist. "I'll make certain of that. Here—take her. Maybe you will be safer with an unconscious sacrifice. Comb out her hair—wash her body. Put on the golden harness—get her ready for the knife."

They took Jean from him and laid her on a marble slab and continued their ministrations. Pandek, scowling deeply, walked to the window and looked out. Beyond and below, was a great open square filled with many people. They milled about a high, central platform upon which sat a throne and a sacrificial block. The block was caked with the blood—the blood of a thousand sacrifices made before the Reformation, centuries before. It had been removed from the square, but had been carefully preserved by a core of fanatics who had never given up hope of the Old Regime coming once again into power; the old, bloody regime that worshiped the robust pagan gods and gave the people great spectacles.

Now the block had been returned; the minds of the people had been inflamed and they awaited the first sacrifice of the New Age—the age in which proud pagan Mars would again demand its rightful place in the sun. Pandek's hand thrilled for the feel of the knife. He thrilled at the thought of driving it home and thus ushering in the New Age.

His mind went, quite naturally, to Fanton, the weak old fool of a leader he had dragged down. It had been a clever coup. Of course, Fanton still had a sizable number of followers, but they had been misled, lied to, cleverly hoodwinked. A little fearful of a slip in his plans, Pandek had not had Fanton slain. He had merely thrown the old fool into a cell to die—had deprived him of rejuvenation.

Perhaps Fanton, was already dead. Pandek wondered. But perhaps not, and with plans having gone forward so smoothly, it was safe to kill the deposed Lord of the Northern Hemisphere.

Pandek turned swiftly and went to see about it.

CHAPTER EIGHT

MAXIS, leading his cavalcade down the prison corridor and carrying the even frailer body of his Emperor, traveled half the breadth of the prison before danger confronted him: three guards loyal to Pandek the usurper and dedicated to his treacherous cause.

Maxis laid the body of Fanton gently upon the floor. Then he stepped over it and made his stand between his Emperor and those who had deserted him. He paid no attention to the two Terrans. He wished them neither harm nor good fortune, they would be of no value in this fight so he forgot them.

The guards, sure of their advantage, moved slowly forward. They knew Maxis and gave him a tribute by taking it for granted he would not retreat. They drew their short, wicked swords, thus forcing Maxis, a man of ethics, to foreswear use of any other weapon even though death faced him.

The Martians moved in from three angles, skillful swordsmen all, and Maxis parried three quick thrusts with a tricky maneuver that left a scratch on the arm of one guard.

It was a gallant parry, worthy of a better reward than certain death. The guards retreated a step, set themselves, and moved in again. Maxis would certainly not be able to repeat the maneuver.

Then there was new, sudden, and devastating action. From the rear of the guards, came a crazed, unarmed juggernaut of destruction; a mad Terran; Bloody, savage-eyed, lethal, he threw himself against the flank of the advancing trio, locked an arm around his throat, and with leverage obtained by wrapping his legs around the Martian's body, snapped the ugly head at the base of the spine.

The Martian fell with the Terran under him. As Tommy cried, "Rex—Rex! Where did you come from?" the Terran had disentangled himself from the corpse and was engaging a second guard. Stunned by the suddenness of the attacks, the guard was easy prey for the Terran's death grip. A second spine snapped and as the Terran rose, he saw that the third guard had fallen before Maxis' sword.

Maxis said. "Your aid was indeed timely."

Rex wiped blood from his face and advanced like a great cat. "What are you doing with these people?"

Tommy rushed forward. "It's all right, Rex. This is our friend. The old man is the Lord of the North Hemisphere. Maxis is trying to save his life. This is Helen Spencer. They were going to kill her."

Maxis had again taken Fanton in his arms. "We have no time to discuss these things. Find a gun on one of those bodies and follow."

He moved swiftly down the corridor. Tommy and Helen Spencer followed, but Rex strode forward until he was abreast of the Martian. "Where are we going?" There was suspicion and hostility in his voice—as though he suspected a trick.

"I can't go into detail," Maxis said, "but believe me, our chances of survival lie in reaching a ray fountain we call the Place of Eternal Strength. The Emperor's life is at stake and ours also."

As though on cue, two guards appeared from a cross-corridor. Grinning mirthlessly, Rex turned the gun on them. It spat forth a crackling ray that cut them in the middle and brought the upper halves of their bodies toppling to the floor.

"Now lead the way," Rex said.

He killed four more guards before they arrived at the Place of Eternal Strength, shooting them in the back without compunction as he stalked ahead of Rex, clearing the way.

Upon arrival at their destination, Tommy cried, "Why this is the place where my arm was healed. I had a wound and then it was gone!"

MAXIS laid the body of Fanton on a marble couch under the singing colored rays. "Even greater miracles are achieved here," he said. "It heals all ills—even old age. If a spark of life remains in a body, the fountain greatens and strengthens it."

Rex stared in wonder. "Will it revive the dead?"

"No. It will preserve a dead body—cause it to remain perfect for centuries but once life is gone it can never be returned."

"Then this what happened to Professor Spencer. He was killed and placed under this ray."

Maxis nodded sadly. "Brutally murdered. It was Pandek's signal for his great coup. We were caught completely unawares. He acted very cleverly and told us

Fanton had died, refusing rejuvenation, when in truth he had deprived Fanton of the fountain's healing power. Only today did I discover that Fanton still lived."

Rex was staring at the body of the ancient ruler. "How long does the process take?"

"A matter of minutes. Let's only hope that those minutes are afforded us."

"There are still some shots in my gun," Rex said.

They waited, while the body of Fanton seemed to visibly recharge itself. Two guards appeared. Rex killed them.

"How was this rebellion allowed to get started?" he asked.

There was a grim look upon Maxis' face. "Through laxness. Through carelessness. From plugging our ears against the sound of treacherous undercurrents. From feeling that young hotheads were basically sound and would not arrange their own destruction and ours too."

"This Pandek you speak of—he planned to move against the Terrans to the south?"

"He still plans it. He has vowed to wipe every alien from the planet and establish a new age of Martian resurgence."

"The Martians would be annihilated."

"Pandek is willing to gamble on that."

"He must be insane," Rex said.

"It began when Fanton advocated a change in Martian policy. For centuries, ever since the Terrans came, our course has been one of proud isolation. The policy was instituted centuries ago by ill-advised leaders and Fanton carried it on against his better judgment.

When he began talking of a reversal, the underground mutiny gained in strength."

"Will saving Fanton's life stop the rebellion?"

"This thing we do is only a feeble step in the right direction. Even with Fanton strong and healthy, we may not be able to win."

"What is this sacrifice business?"

"It is supposed to take place in the public square. An old and barbaric rite in which a maiden is slain and the people file by and bathe their hands in her blood. It will be the signal for the final act of overthrow—when the rebels come into the open and slay all who remain faithful to Fanton."

A new voice spoke. The two men turned. Fanton was sitting on the edge of the marble couch. Helen and Tommy were staring at him.

Fanton's words were for Maxis. "You have done well. If I'd known before where loyalty lay, things might have been different."

Maxis dropped to one knee. He bowed his head. "My lord."

"No time for this. I must get to the Council."

"It will be very dangerous."

"But the uprising must be beaten down. The Council is still loyal. They must see that I am alive."

Rex said, "I think you'll find—"

Fanton waved him to silence. "We must hurry."

AS the group left the Place of Eternal Strength, Maxis said, "Perhaps they will have to be assembled. If they are not in session."

"They must be in session!"

On the trip to the Amphitheater of the Gods, two rebels were killed and one loyal Martian added to the cavalcade. As they moved into the great hall, Fanton said, "They are here…"

This appeared to be true. The seats flanking the central throne were still occupied. The throne itself was vacant. Immediately upon entering the great hall, Rex ran forward and climbed to the tier of benches. The council members sat silent, unmoving. Rex pushed the body of the nearest one. It tumbled off the bench like a sack of grain and fell to the floor.

Fanton paled. "What does this mean?"

"They're all dead," Rex replied.

"When we were here before I noticed that none of them moved nor spoke. This is the work of a madman—Pandek. This is his joke. He rules all alone."

Maxis said, "You will have to try and escape, my Lord. You must get to the Terrans and tell your story."

Fanton considered. "If I run like a coward, thousands of loyal Martians will die. Their blood will be on my hands."

"That's not true," Rex said, sharply.

Further talk was interrupted by the sound of men approaching at a run. Fanton turned and pointed. "Behind that pillar! There is a small door that leads to an observatory platform above the square. Only my father knew of the stairway behind the wall."

Fanton pressed a carved leaf in a decoration on the pillar and a small section of the seemingly unbroken wall moved inward. Fanton entered and the rest followed with Rex and Maxis and the new recruit bringing up the rear.

Maxis said, "I will stay here and fight. I'm tired of running away."

Rex dragged him into the opening. "Don't be a fool. There's a time to fight and a time to run. This is a time to run."

As the wall-section slid back into place, Fanton indicated a stairway a short distance down the narrow corridor. Rex said to Maxis. "You go on ahead, to guard Fanton. This new man and I will stay here in case Fanton and his father weren't the only ones who knew about that opening. I think whoever was coming heard us leave."

Maxis was prepared to object. He hesitated, watching Fanton, Tommy and Helen move up the circular stairway. "Go ahead," Rex snapped. "You don't know who may be up there."

Scowling, Maxis turned suddenly and took the stairs three at a time.

Rex and the loyal Martian had a short wait. The sound of the others had scarcely died out above, when the panel opened again. "I was right," Rex whispered. "Stand on the other side."

The two defenders had the advantage of a comparatively dim interior; that, and the remaining charges in Rex's gun. Three guards crowded into the narrow passageway.

As they saw Rex standing by the stairway, he dropped to the floor and fired at an upward angle. His lethal charges cut the two forward guards to pieces.

The third one, though confused, was more alert. He also had a gun and looked desperately around for a target. The loyal Martian thrust viciously with his sword.

He missed. The guard danced away. Rex brought his gun around, but hesitated with the loyal Martian in his range of fire. When he maneuvered a clear shot, he pressed the switch. Nothing happened. The gun was empty.

In the meantime, the guard brought his gun around to bear on the Martian. The later made a second desperate thrust. It went home but only as the Martian fell dead from the guard's last shot. Rex got to his feet, wiping sweat from his face.

And at that moment, Pandek stepped into the passageway.

Instantly, Rex leaped for the fallen guard's gun. Pandek smiled contemptuously and kicked it far down the passageway. Pandek apprised the situation swiftly. He said, "Pick up the sword, Terran scum."

Without reply, Rex bent down and did as directed.

"Are you skilled in its use?" Pandek asked.

"I never had one in my hand before."

Pandek raised his own sword, identical to the one Rex held. "Then I'm afraid the contest will be rather unequal," he said and moved toward Rex. "On guard... It will be a great pleasure to kill you."

Rex took a backward step. He was no match for Pandek with these weapons. Pandek would be a master at close swordsmanship. This had to be true. Otherwise Pandek would not be so eager to engage him.

Rex thought of the headquarters on Earth; of Professor Spencer, so still, so peaceful in that box. So dead. Would he go back to Terra the same way?

With Fanton's hiding place known to Pandek, the rebellion seemed assured of success—as certain as his own death at Pandek's hands.

He took another backward step.

CHAPTER NINE

JEAN was ready for the sacrifice. She had been dressed in a rich golden harness and wore golden manacles on her wrists. She had waited in the room with the sound of the crowds in the great court below rising in volume as their impatience increased.

Finally a door opened. A tall resplendent figure entered. He wore a jeweled cloak that swept the floor. A hideous golden mask covered his face.

There were two attending priests with Jean. They dropped to their knees and lowered their eyes. One of them intoned, "Great Pandek. Lord of the Northern Hemisphere. The sacrifice is ready for your knife."

The room grew hazy before Jean's eyes. It spun in a sickening swirl as she slipped to the floor in a dead faint.

When she regained consciousness, Jean found herself under an archway in the court below. The great square was jammed with howling Martians. A long red carpet stretched from the archway to the platform in the center of the square. The sting of a sharp odor in her nostrils told Jean how she had been revived.

A priest on either side now supported her. They moved forward from the building toward the platform. Evidently, she could either walk or be dragged. She preferred to walk. She raised her head high and matched the priest's step for step.

The crowd pressed close to the red carpet on either side. Unbroken lines of guards held the Martians back. To Jean, they seemed things out of a nightmare.

They reached the steps leading up to the platform. Five steps. She counted them as she ascended.

The marble block.

The priests laid her along its length. The golden manacles were removed. Each priest took an arm and held her to the slab with the tall masked figure raising his knife and looking down at her. The knife arched.

Then, halfway in its descent toward her bared breast, it stopped. The masked figure looked upward toward the high wall of the building He shrank backward— pointed with the knife as he cringed away.

A dramatic gesture that turned every eye in the square toward a small balcony high on the wall. A cry went up. A single word.

"Fanton!"

The true Lord of the Northern Hemisphere stood with his arms outstretched imperiously over the crowd below. He held this position until the roaring died away and a whisper could have been heard in the great square. Then he spoke.

"Hear your Emperor now! You have been lied to by those whom would destroy you. You have been told I was dead. I am not dead. You have been told that a new order would prevail among you. This is an old, archaic order that brought only blood and suffering in its time. I tell you now that those who spoke thus were traitors. Traitors who sought to exploit your suffering to their cruel ends. The leader of these traitors was Pandek, a prince I trusted. I now declare his life forfeit and say to you that he will be executed in public at this hour one day hence. Return now to your homes and have done with this madness. I, your Emperor, command each of you personally. You who are vested with authority, return to your duties."

The sonorous voice ceased and Jean felt herself being raised from the marble slab. She opened her eyes. The golden mask had been lifted from the face of the executioner. He had dropped the knife and now he held a sword in his hand.

It was Maxis.

He whispered, "Under the platform, quick! There is an underground passage back into the palace. You will be safe."

Jean was bewildered. As she descended she saw that the crowd had surged backward, leaving an open space between the platform and the palace. Maxis turned and ran toward the open space.

A small group of Martians was running forward from the building. They were led by Pandek with a sword in his hand. From another doorway, Rex ran to join Maxis. He was unarmed.

One of Pandek's group turned and swerved out to intercept him. Like a great cat, Rex crouched, waiting. The Martian moved in. Rex went under the vicious swipe of the Martian's sword and caught the Martian's arm and spun him around. Before the Martian could recover his balance, there was an arm around his throat—pressure on his spine. He screamed as his spine snapped. Rex raced on and joined Maxis.

THE guards in the square had now chosen sides. A few rallied behind Pandek. By far the majority took their stand behind Maxis. Their number doomed the smaller group.

But Maxis held up his hands. "Stand back! All of you... Come forward, Pandek. You think so highly of your swordsman's skill. Let me see the proof. Just we two."

Pandek was not slow in accepting the challenge. He came forward and the two Martians circled cautiously in the open space between the two opposing forces.

Pandek seemed the better of the two. Maxis fought mainly on the defensive, his play unspectacular, which made Pandek's thrusts seem all the more brilliant.

Pandek evidently felt any retreat was a mark against him. Not so with Maxis. He retreated whenever it was made necessary by Pandek's able thrusts. Pandek sneered. Maxis fought stolidly, doggedly.

Until Pandek made the mistake of losing regard for his foe's ability. He thrust smartly and did not maintain the balance necessary for retreat in case of quick counter attack.

The counterattack came. Suddenly Maxis' blade was everywhere. Pandek started to retreat in order to regain his balance and reassume domination of the match.

Maxis never gave him a chance to do this.

Pandek was a scant second too late in parrying a thrust to balance himself for the next. He fell.

Maxis moved in swiftly. For a moment he stayed his thrust...hoping. And what he hoped for, came to pass. Pandek's courage broke. With terror in his eyes, the fallen Martian shouted. "Stop! I am of royal blood. You don't dare kill me!"

Maxis smiled and drove his blade home.

As he drew it forth, he glanced at Pandek's waiting group. Brave men all, who had espoused the losing cause openly. To a man they were throwing down their swords, their eyes on the dead Pandek, contempt on their faces. The contempt of men who suddenly realized they had been led by a coward. Men who were ashamed.

Maxis sheathed his blade and looked up to where Fanton, Lord of the Northern Hemisphere raised his hand in salute.

Maxis bowed. Then he turned to Rex. He said, "It is over, my friend. The fuse has been snuffed in time. We will be eternally in your gratitude."

"It's the other way around. We're getting out of this little affair with whole skins. That's something to be really thankful for."

* * *

(From the diary of Tommy Wilks)

What a story I'll have to tell! I guess I'm about the luckiest kid on Mars right now because when we get back, they're going to let me tell what happened! I've got it all written down so I won't forget anything. I've got it up to the time we left Rex and the Martian in the passageway behind the wall. Rex didn't tell me all that happened but when Maxis got back there, after hearing the noise, he found Pandek on the floor unconscious. Rex said Pandek came at him with a sword and he was pretty sure Pandek would kill him but Pandek missed a thrust and Rex got in a lucky grab and pushed a nerve on Pandek's neck. He made it sound very easy but I'll bet Rex is about the best nerve fighter in the world. That's what they call men who can kill with nothing but their bare hands.

Anyhow, they brought Pandek upstairs and Maxis wanted to kill him. But Fanton said no—that Pandek should be kept alive until the rebellion was over—if it ever was.

They talked about what they'd do, but Fanton made the final decision because he was the Emperor. He said he wanted to reveal himself to the people at a dramatic moment because that was what had an affect on crowds. He decided the most dramatic moment would be while the knife was raised over Jean.

So they took Pandek to a room and tied him up and Maxis took his place. Maxis' job was to call the crowd's attention to Fanton at the right instant to heighten the dramatic effect. He was also suppose to look scared to death so the crowd wouldn't swing Pandek's side against the Emperor.

It all worked swell except for one thing. Some traitor guards came and let Pandek out. If Pandek had gone after Fanton, it all might have ended differently. That's what Rex said. But Pandek got rattled and went after Maxis instead. Maxis killed him even though Pandek was a much better swordsman.

Now to me, that doesn't make any sense. I asked Rex about that but he just smiled and said Pandek was better than Maxis except for one thing. Guts. That's a funny term that means courage. I wonder where Rex heard it. Probably on Earth.

Anyhow, everything is fine, now. The people are behind Fanton and he's coming back to New Iowa with us and wants to go on to Terra for a good-will visit. He wants to open the northern country to Terrans and trade scientific secrets.

Right now I'm in a room they gave me to sleep in while we're here. I saw Jean and Rex walking in the garden down below. He was kissing her.

Or maybe it was the other way around.

THE END

If you've enjoyed this book, you will not want to miss these terrific titles…

ARMCHAIR SCI-FI, FANTASY, & HORROR DOUBLE NOVELS, $12.95 each

D-1   **THE GALAXY RAIDERS** by William P. McGivern
         SPACE STATION #1 by Frank Belknap Long

D-2   **THE PROGRAMMED PEOPLE** by Jack Sharkey
         SLAVES OF THE CRYSTAL BRAIN by William Carter Sawtelle

D-3   **YOU'RE ALL ALONE** by Fritz Leiber
         THE LIQUID MAN by Bernard C. Gilford

D-4   **CITADEL OF THE STAR LORDS** by Edmund Hamilton
         VOYAGE TO ETERNITY by Milton Lesser

D-5   **IRON MEN OF VENUS** by Don Wilcox
         THE MAN WITH ABSOLUTE MOTION by Noel Loomis

D-6   **WHO SOWS THE WIND…** by Rog Phillips
         THE PUZZLE PLANET by Robert A. W. Lowndes

D-7   **PLANET OF DREAD** by Murray Leinster
         TWICE UPON A TIME by Charles L. Fontenay

D-8   **THE TERROR OUT OF SPACE** by Dwight V. Swain
         QUEST OF THE GOLDEN APE by Ivar Jorgensen and Adam Chase

D-9   **SECRET OF MARRACOTT DEEP** by Henry Slesar
         PAWN OF THE BLACK FLEET by Mark Clifton.

D-10   **BEYOND THE RINGS OF SATURN** by Robert Moore Williams
         A MAN OBSESSED by Alan E. Nourse

ARMCHAIR SCIENCE FICTION CLASSICS, $12.95 each

C-1   **THE GREEN MAN**
         by Harold M. Sherman

C-2   **A TRACE OF MEMORY**
         By Keith Laumer

C-3   **INTO PLUTONIAN DEPTHS**
         by Stanton A. Coblentz

ARMCHAIR MASTERS OF SCIENCE FICTION SERIES, $16.95 each

M-1   **MASTERS OF SCIENCE FICTION, Vol. One**
         Bryce Walton—"Dark of the Moon" and other tales

M-2   **MASTERS OF SCIENCE FICTION, Vol. Two**
         Jerome Bixby—"One Way Street" and other tales

If you've enjoyed this book, you will not want to miss these terrific titles…

ARMCHAIR SCI-FI & HORROR DOUBLE NOVELS, $12.95 each

D-11   **PERIL OF THE STARMEN** by Kris Neville
THE STRANGE INVASION by Murray Leinster

D-12   **THE STAR LORD** by Boyd Ellanby
CAPTIVES OF THE FLAME by Samuel R. Delany

D-13   **MEN OF THE MORNING STAR** by Edmund Hamilton
PLANET FOR PLUNDER by Hal Clement and Sam Merwin, Jr.

D-14   **ICE CITY OF THE GORGON** by Chester S. Geier and Richard Shaver
WHEN THE WORLD TOTTERED by Lester Del Rey

D-15   **WORLDS WITHOUT END** by Clifford D. Simak
THE LAVENDER VINE OF DEATH by Don Wilcox

D-16   **SHADOW ON THE MOON** by Joe Gibson
ARMAGEDDON EARTH by Geoff St. Reynard

D-17   **THE GIRL WHO LOVED DEATH** by Paul W. Fairman
SLAVE PLANET by Laurence M. Janifer

D-18   **SECOND CHANCE** by J. F. Bone
MISSION TO A DISTANT STAR by Frank Belknap Long

D-19   **THE SYNDIC** by C. M. Kornbluth
FLIGHT TO FOREVER by Poul Anderson

D-20   **SOMEWHERE I'LL FIND YOU** by Milton Lesser
THE TIME ARMADA by Fox B. Holden

ARMCHAIR SCIENCE FICTION CLASSICS, $12.95 each

C-4   **CORPUS EARTHLING**
by Louis Charbonneau

C-5   **THE TIME DISSOLVER**
by Jerry Sohl

C-6   **WEST OF THE SUN**
by Edgar Pangborn

ARMCHAIR SCIENCE FICTION & HORROR GEMS SERIES, $12.95 each

G-1   **SCIENCE FICTION GEMS, Vol. One**
Isaac Asimov and others

G-2   **HORROR GEMS, Vol. One**
Carl Jacobi and others

If you've enjoyed this book, you will not want to miss these terrific titles…

ARMCHAIR SCI-FI, FANTASY, & HORROR DOUBLE NOVELS, $12.95 each

D-21 **EMPIRE OF EVIL** by Robert Arnette
THE SIGN OF THE TIGER by Alan E. Nourse & J. A. Meyer

D-22 **OPERATION SQUARE PEG** by Frank Belknap Long
ENCHANTRESS OF VENUS by Leigh Brackett

D-23 **THE LIFE WATCH** by Lester Del Rey
CREATURES OF THE ABYSS by Murray Leinster

D-24 **LEGION OF LAZARUS** by Edmond Hamilton
STAR HUNTER by Andre Norton

D-25 **EMPIRE OF WOMEN** by John Fletcher
ONE OF OUR CITIES IS MISSING by Irving Cox

D-26 **THE WRONG SIDE OF PARADISE** by Raymond F. Jones
THE INVOLUNTARY IMMORTALS by Rog Phillips

D-27 **EARTH QUARTER** by Damon Knight
ENVOY TO NEW WORLDS by Keith Laumer

D-28 **SLAVES TO THE METAL HORDE** by Milton Lesser
HUNTERS OUT OF TIME by Joseph E. Kelleam

D-29 **RX JUPITER SAVE US** by Ward Moore
BEWARE THE USURPERS by Geoff St. Reynard

D-30 **SECRET OF THE SERPENT** by Don Wilcox
CRUSADE ACROSS THE VOID by Dwight V. Swain

ARMCHAIR SCIENCE FICTION CLASSICS, $12.95 each

C-7 **THE SHAVER MYSTERY, Book One**
by Richard S. Shaver

C-8 **THE SHAVER MYSTERY, Book Two**
by Richard S. Shaver

C-9 **MURDER IN SPACE** by David V. Reed
by David V. Reed

ARMCHAIR MASTERS OF SCIENCE FICTION SERIES, $16.95 each

M-3 **MASTERS OF SCIENCE FICTION, Vol. Three**
Robert Sheckley, "The Perfect Woman" and other tales

M-4 **MASTERS OF SCIENCE FICTION, Vol. Four**
Mack Reynolds, "Stowaway" and other tales

If you've enjoyed this book, you will not want to miss these terrific titles...

ARMCHAIR SCI-FI & HORROR DOUBLE NOVELS, $12.95 each

D-31   **A HOAX IN TIME** by Keith Laumer
INSIDE EARTH by Poul Anderson

D-32   **TERROR STATION** by Dwight V. Swain
THE WEAPON FROM ETERNITY by Dwight V. Swain

D-33   **THE SHIP FROM INFINITY** by Edmond Hamilton
TAKEOFF by C. M. Kornbluth

D-34   **THE METAL DOOM** by David H. Keller
TWELVE TIMES ZERO by Howard Browne

D-35   **HUNTERS OUT OF SPACE** by Joseph Kelleam
INVASION FROM THE DEEP by Paul W. Fairman,

D-36   **THE BEES OF DEATH** by Robert Moore Williams
A PLAGUE OF PYTHONS by Frederick Pohl

D-37   **THE LORDS OF QUARMALL** by Fritz Leiber and Harry Fischer
BEACON TO ELSEWHERE by James H. Schmitz

D-38   **BEYOND PLUTO** by John S. Campbell
ARTERY OF FIRE by Thomas N. Scortia

D-39   **SPECIAL DELIVERY** by Kris Neville
NO TIME FOR TOFFEE by Charles F. Meyers

D-40   **JUNGLE IN THE SKY** by Milton Lesser
RECALLED TO LIFE by Robert Silverberg

ARMCHAIR SCIENCE FICTION CLASSICS, $12.95 each

C-10   **MARS IS MY DESTINATION**
by Frank Belknap Long

C-11   **SPACE PLAGUE**
by George O. Smith

C-12   **SO SHALL YE REAP**
by Rog Phillips

ARMCHAIR SCIENCE FICTION & HORROR GEMS SERIES, $12.95 each

G-3   **SCIENCE FICTION GEMS, Vol. Two**
James Blish and others

G-4   **HORROR GEMS, Vol. Two**
Joseph Payne Brennan and others

If you've enjoyed this book, you will not want to miss these terrific titles...

ARMCHAIR SCI-FI, FANTASY, & HORROR DOUBLE NOVELS, $12.95 each

D-41   **FULL CYCLE** by Clifford D. Simak
IT WAS THE DAY OF THE ROBOT by Frank Belknap Long

D-42   **THIS CROWDED EARTH** by Robert Bloch
REIGN OF THE TELEPUPPETS by Daniel Galouye

D-43   **THE CRISPIN AFFAIR** by Jack Sharkey
THE RED HELL OF JUPITER by Paul Ernst

D-44   **PLANET OF DREAD** by Dwight V. Swain
WE THE MACHINE by Gerald Vance

D-45   **THE STAR HUNTER** by Edmond Hamilton
THE ALIEN by Raymond F. Jones

D-46   **WORLD OF IF** by Rog Phillips
SLAVE RAIDERS FROM MERCURY by Don Wilcox

D-47   **THE ULTIMATE PERIL** by Robert Abernathy
PLANET OF SHAME by Bruce Elliot

D-48   **THE FLYING EYES** by J. Hunter Holly
SOME FABULOUS YONDER by Phillip Jose Farmer

D-49   **THE COSMIC BUNGLARS** by Geoff St. Reynard
THE BUTTONED SKY by Geoff St. Reynard

D-50   **TYRANTS OF TIME** by Milton Lesser
PARIAH PLANET by Murray Leinster

ARMCHAIR SCIENCE FICTION CLASSICS, $12.95 each

C-13   **SUNKEN WORLD**
by Stanton A. Coblentz

C-14   **THE LAST VIAL**
by Sam McClatchie, M. D.

C-15   **WE WHO SURVIVED (THE FIFTH ICE AGE)**
by Sterling Noel

ARMCHAIR MASTERS OF SCIENCE FICTION SERIES, $16.95 each

MS-5   **MASTERS OF SCIENCE FICTION, Vol. Five**
Winston K. Marks—Test Colony and other tales

MS-6   **MASTERS OF SCIENCE FICTION, Vol. Six**
Fritz Leiber—Deadly Moon and other tales

If you've enjoyed this book, you will not want to miss these terrific titles...

ARMCHAIR SCI-FI & HORROR DOUBLE NOVELS, $12.95 each

D-51   **A GOD NAMED SMITH** by Henry Slesar
WORLDS OF THE IMPERIUM by Keith Laumer

D-52   **CRAIG'S BOOK** by Don Wilcox
EDGE OF THE KNIFE by H. Beam Piper

D-53   **THE SHINING CITY** by Rena M. Vale
THE RED PLANET by Russ Winterbotham

D-54   **THE MAN WHO LIVED TWICE** by Rog Phillips
VALLEY OF THE CROEN by Lee Tarbell

D-55   **OPERATION DISASTER** by Milton Lesser
LAND OF THE DAMNED by Berkeley Livingston

D-56   **CAPTIVE OF THE CENTAURIANESS** by Poul Anderson
A PRINCESS OF MARS by Edgar Rice Burroughs

D-57   **THE NON-STATISTICAL MAN** by Raymond F. Jones
MISSION FROM MARS by Rick Conroy

D-58   **INTRUDERS FROM THE STARS** by Ross Rocklynne
FLIGHT OF THE STARLING by Chester S. Geier

D-59   **COSMIC SABOTEUR** by Frank M. Robinson
LOOK TO THE STARS by Willard Hawkins

D-60   **THE MOON IS HELL!** by John W. Campbell, Jr.
THE GREEN WORLD by Hal Clement

ARMCHAIR SCIENCE FICTION CLASSICS, $12.95 each

C-16   **THE SHAVER MYSTERY, Book Three**
by Richard S. Shaver

C-17   **THE PLANET STRAPPERS**
by Raymond Z. Gallun

C-18   **THE FOURTH "R"**
by George O. Smith

ARMCHAIR SCIENCE FICTION & HORROR GEMS SERIES, $12.95 each

G-5   **SCIENCE FICTION GEMS, Vol. Three**
C. M. Kornbluth and others

G-6   **HORROR GEMS, Vol. Three**
August Derleth and others

If you've enjoyed this book, you will not want to miss these terrific titles…

ARMCHAIR SCI-FI & HORROR DOUBLE NOVELS, $12.95 each

D-61   **THE MAN WHO STOPPED AT NOTHING** by Paul W. Fairman
TEN FROM INFINITY by Ivar Jorgensen

D-62   **WORLDS WITHIN** by Rog Phillips
THE SLAVE by C.M. Kornbluth

D-63   **SECRET OF THE BLACK PLANET** by Milton Lesser
THE OUTCASTS OF SOLAR III by Emmett McDowell

D-64   **WEB OF THE WORLDS** by Harry Harrison and Katherine MacLean
RULE GOLDEN by Damon Knight

D-65   **TEN TO THE STARS** by Raymond Z. Gallun
THE CONQUERORS by David H. Keller, M. D.

D-66   **THE HORDE FROM INFINITY** by Dwight V. Swain
THE DAY THE EARTH FROZE by Gerald Hatch

D-67   **THE WAR OF THE WORLDS** by H. G. Wells
THE TIME MACHINE by H. G. Wells

D-68   **STARCOMBERS** by Edmond Hamilton
THE YEAR WHEN STARDUST FELL by Raymond F. Jones

D-69   **HOCUS-POCUS UNIVERSE** by Jack Williamson
QUEEN OF THE PANTHER WORLD by Berkeley Livingston

D-70   **BATTERING RAMS OF SPACE** by Don Wilcox
DOOMSDAY WING by George H. Smith

ARMCHAIR SCIENCE FICTION & FANTASY CLASSICS, $12.95 each

C-19   **EMPIRE OF JEGGA**
by David V. Reed

C-20   **THE TOMORROW PEOPLE**
by Judith Merril

C-21   **THE MAN FROM YESTERDAY**
by Howard Browne as by Lee Francis

C-22   **THE TIME TRADERS**
by Andre Norton

C-23   **ISLANDS OF SPACE**
by John W. Campbell

C-24   **THE GALAXY PRIMES**
by E. E. "Doc" Smith

If you've enjoyed this book, you will not want to miss these terrific titles...

ARMCHAIR SCI-FI & HORROR DOUBLE NOVELS, $12.95 each

D-71   **THE DEEP END** by Gregory Luce
TO WATCH BY NIGHT by Robert Moore Williams

D-72   **SWORDSMAN OF LOST TERRA** by Poul Anderson
PLANET OF GHOSTS by David V. Reed

D-73   **MOON OF BATTLE** by J. J. Allerton
THE MUTANT WEAPON by Murray Leinster

D-74   **OLD SPACEMEN NEVER DIE!** John Jakes
RETURN TO EARTH by Bryan Berry

D-75   **THE THING FROM UNDERNEATH** by Milton Lesser
OPERATION INTERSTELLAR by George O. Smith

D-76   **THE BURNING WORLD** by Algis Budrys
FOREVER IS TOO LONG by Chester S. Geier

D-77   **THE COSMIC JUNKMAN** by Rog Phillips
THE ULTIMATE WEAPON by John W. Campbell

D-78   **THE TIES OF EARTH** by James H. Schmitz
CUE FOR QUIET by Thomas L. Sherred

D-79   **SECRET OF THE MARTIANS** by Paul W. Fairman
THE VARIABLE MAN by Philip K. Dick

D-80   **THE GREEN GIRL** by Jack Williamson
THE ROBOT PERIL by Don Wilcox

ARMCHAIR SCIENCE FICTION CLASSICS, $12.95 each

C-25   **THE STAR KINGS**
by Edmond Hamilton

C-26   **NOT IN SOLITUDE**
by Kenneth Gantz

C-32   **PROMETHEUS II**
by S. J. Byrne

ARMCHAIR SCIENCE FICTION & HORROR GEMS SERIES, $12.95 each

G-7   **SCIENCE FICTION GEMS, Vol. Seven**
Jack Sharkey and others

G-8   **HORROR GEMS, Vol. Eight**
Seabury Quinn and others

JUST A MAN WHO LIKED TO TINKER...

He was always tinkering with things, fixing things, everything from clocks to refrigerators to vidsenders…and to destinies. But one thing was certain, he had no business in the world of the future, where the calculators simply couldn't handle him. On one hand he was Earth's only hope…and on the other hand he was its sure failure.

Join science fiction maestro Philip K. Dick for one of his earliest works. "The Variable Man" was first published in the September issue of "Space Science Fiction" magazine, all the way back in 1953. Even at this early stage of his career, Dick's talent for writing was obvious in this strange tale of strange man in the far-off future.

ABOUT PHILIP K. DICK...

Philip K. Dick was a native of Chicago, born there on December 16th, 1928. In a career devoted primarily to the science fiction genre, Dick began writing in the early 1950s. His first published story was "Beyond Lies the Wub," first published in the July, 1952 issue of *Planet Stories*. During the '50s and '60s, Dick was a sci-fi workhorse, turning out countless short stories and many novels. Most of his early novels were published in Ace Books' Double Novel Series.

During his long, brilliant career, Dick often employed sociological, metaphysical, and political themes. His novels and stories were often dominated by monopolistic entities, totalitarian governments, and altered states. Later in his career, Dick's works often focused on theology, of which he had a personal interest in after going through a number of hallucinatory experiences in the 1970s.

In 2005, Time magazine named Dick's 1969 novel, "Ubik" one of the one hundred greatest English-language novels published since 1923.

Philip K. Dick passed away from the effects of a stroke,on March 2nd, 1982

THE
VARIABLE
MAN

By
PHILIP K. DICK

ARMCHAIR FICTION
PO Box 4369, Medford, Oregon   97501-0168

CHAPTER ONE

He fixed things—clocks, refrigerators, vidsenders and destinies. But he had no business in the future, where the calculators could not handle him. He was Earth's only hope—and its sure failure!

Security Commissioner Reinhart rapidly climbed the front steps and entered the Council building. Council guards stepped quickly aside and he entered the familiar place of great whirring machines. His thin face rapt, eyes alight with emotion, Reinhart gazed intently up at the central SRB computer, studying its reading.

"Straight gain for the last quarter," observed Kaplan, the lab organizer. He grinned proudly, as if personally responsible. "Not bad, Commissioner."

"We're catching up to them," Reinhart retorted. "But too damn slowly. We must finally go over—and soon."

Kaplan was in a talkative mood. "We design new offensive weapons, they counter with improved defenses. And nothing is actually made! Continual improvement, but neither we nor Centaurus can stop designing long enough to stabilize for production."

"It will end," Reinhart stated coldly, "as soon as Terra turns out a weapon for which Centaurus can build no defense."

"Every weapon has a defense. Design and discord. Immediate obsolescence. Nothing lasts long enough to—"

"What we count on is the *lag*," Reinhart broke in, annoyed. His hard gray eyes bored into the lab organizer and Kaplan slunk back. "The time lag between our offensive design and their counter development. The lag varies." He waved impatiently toward the massed banks of SRB machines. "As you well know."

At this moment, 9:30 AM, May 7, 2136, the statistical ratio on the SRB machines stood at 21-17 on the Centauran side of the ledger. All facts considered, the odds favored a successful repulsion by Proxima Centaurus of a Terran military attack. The ratio was based on the total information known to the SRB machines, on a gestalt of the vast flow of data that poured in endlessly from all sectors of the Sol and Centaurus systems.

21-17 on the Centauran side. But a month ago it had been 24-18 in the enemy's favor. Things were improving, slowly but steadily. Centaurus, older and less virile than Terra, was unable to match Terra's rate of technocratic advance. Terra was pulling ahead.

"If we went to war now," Reinhart said thoughtfully, "we would lose. We're not far enough along to risk an overt attack." A harsh, ruthless glow twisted across his handsome features, distorting them into a stern mask. "But the odds are moving in our favor. Our offensive designs are gradually gaining on their defenses."

"Let's hope the war comes soon," Kaplan agreed. "We're all on edge. This damn waiting…."

The war would come soon. Reinhart knew it intuitively. The air was full of tension, the *elan*. He left the SRB rooms and hurried down the corridor to his own elaborately guarded office in the Security wing. It wouldn't be long. He could practically feel the hot breath of destiny on his neck—for him a pleasant feeling. His thin lips set in a humorless smile, showing an even line of white teeth against his tanned skin. It made him feel good, all right. He'd been working at it a long time.

First contact, a hundred years earlier, had ignited instant conflict between Proxima Centauran outposts and exploring Terran raiders. Flash fights, sudden eruptions of fire and energy beams.

And then the long, dreary years of inaction between enemies where contact required years of travel, even at nearly the speed of light. The two systems were evenly matched. Screen against screen. Warship against power station. The Centauran Empire surrounded Terra, an iron ring that couldn't be broken, rusty and corroded as it was. Radical new weapons had to be conceived, if Terra was to break out.

Through the windows of his office, Reinhart could see endless buildings and streets, Terrans hurrying back and forth. Bright specks that were commute ships, little eggs that carried businessmen and white-collar workers around. The huge transport tubes that shot masses of workmen to factories and labor camps from their housing units. All these people, waiting to break out. Waiting for the day.

Reinhart snapped on his vidscreen, the confidential channel. "Give me Military Designs," he ordered sharply.

He sat tense, his wiry body taut, as the vidscreen warmed into life. Abruptly he was facing the hulking image of Peter Sherikov, director of the vast network of labs under the Ural Mountains.

Sherikov's great bearded features hardened as he recognized Reinhart. His bushy black eyebrows pulled up in a sullen line. "What do you want? You know I'm busy. We have too much work to do, as it is. Without being bothered by—politicians."

"I'm dropping over your way," Reinhart answered lazily. He adjusted the cuff of his immaculate gray cloak. "I want a full description of your work and whatever progress you've made."

"You'll find a regular departmental report plate filed in the usual way, around your office someplace. If you'll refer to that you'll know exactly what we—"

"I'm not interested in that. I want to *see* what you're doing. And I expect you to be prepared to describe your work fully. I'll be there shortly. Half an hour."

Reinhart cut the circuit. Sherikov's heavy features dwindled and faded. Reinhart relaxed, letting his breath out. Too bad he had to work with Sherikov. He had never liked the man. The big Polish scientist was an individualist, refusing to integrate himself with society. Independent, atomistic in outlook. He held concepts of the individual as an end, diametrically contrary to the accepted organic state Weltansicht.

But Sherikov was the leading research scientist, in charge of the Military Designs Department. And on Designs the whole future of Terra depended. Victory over Centaurus—or more waiting, bottled up in the Sol System, surrounded by a rotting, hostile Empire, now sinking into ruin and decay, yet still strong.

Reinhart got quickly to his feet and left the office. He hurried down the hall and out of the Council building.

A few minutes later he was heading across the mid-morning sky in his high-speed cruiser, toward the Asiatic land-mass, the vast Ural mountain range. Toward the Military Designs labs.

Sherikov met him at the entrance. "Look here, Reinhart. Don't think you're going to order me around. I'm not going to—"

"Take it easy." Reinhart fell into step beside the bigger man. They passed through the check and into the auxiliary labs. "No immediate coercion will be exerted over you or your staff. You're free to continue your work as you see fit—for the present. Let's get this straight. My concern is to integrate your work with our total social needs. As long as your work is sufficiently productive—"

Reinhart stopped in his tracks.

"Pretty, isn't he?" Sherikov said ironically.

"What the hell is it?

"Icarus, we call him. Remember the Greek myth? The legend of Icarus. Icarus flew.... This Icarus is going to fly, one of these days." Sherikov shrugged. "You can examine him, if you want. I suppose this is what you came here to see."

Reinhart advanced slowly. "This is the weapon you've been working on?"

"How does he look?"

Rising up in the center of the chamber was a squat metal cylinder, a great ugly cone of dark gray. Technicians circled around it, wiring up the exposed relay banks. Reinhart caught a glimpse of endless tubes and filaments, a maze of wires and terminals and parts criss-crossing each other, layer on layer.

"What is it?" Reinhart perched on the edge of a workbench, leaning his big shoulders against the wall. "An idea of Jamison Hedge—the same man who developed our instantaneous interstellar vidcasts forty years ago. He was trying to find a method of faster than light travel when he was killed, destroyed along with most of his work. After that faster-than-light research was abandoned. It looked as if there were no future in it."

"Wasn't it shown that nothing could travel faster than light?"

"The interstellar vidcasts do! No, Hedge developed a valid faster-than-light drive. He managed to propel an object at fifty times the speed of light. But as the object gained speed, its length began to diminish and its mass increased. This was in line with familiar twentieth-century concepts of mass-energy transformation. We conjectured that as Hedge's object gained velocity it would continue to lose length and gain mass until its length became nil and its mass infinite. Nobody can imagine such an object."

"Go on."

"But what actually occurred is this. Hedge's object continued to lose length and gain mass until it reached the theoretical limit of velocity, the speed of light. At that point the object, still gaining speed, simply ceased to exist. Having no length, it ceased to occupy space. It disappeared. However, the object had not been *destroyed*. It continued on its way, gaining momentum each moment, moving in an arc across the galaxy, away from the Sol system. Hedge's object entered some other realm of being, beyond our powers of conception. The next phase of Hedge's experiment consisted in a search for some way to slow the faster-than-light object down, back to a sub-faster-than-light speed, hence back into our universe. This counter principle was eventually worked out."

"With what result?"

"The death of Hedge and destruction of most of his equipment. His experimental object, in re-entering the space-time universe, came into being in space already occupied by matter. Possessing an incredible mass, just below infinity level, Hedge's object exploded in a titanic cataclysm. It was obvious that no space travel was possible with such a drive. Virtually all space contains *some* matter. To re-enter space would bring automatic destruction. Hedge had found his faster-than-light drive and his counter principle, but no one before this has been able to put them to any use."

Reinhart walked over toward the great metal cylinder. Sherikov jumped down and followed him. "I don't get it," Reinhart said. "You said the principle is no good for space travel."

"That's right."

"What's this for, then? If the ship explodes as soon as it returns to our universe—"

"This is not a ship." Sherikov grinned slyly. "Icarus is the first practical application of Hedge's principles. Icarus is a bomb."

"So this is our weapon," Reinhart said. "A bomb. An immense bomb."

"A bomb, moving at a velocity greater than light. A bomb which will not exist in our universe. The Centaurans won't be able to detect or stop it. How could they? As soon as it passes the speed of light it will cease to exist—beyond all detection."

"But—"

"Icarus will be launched outside the lab, on the surface. He will align himself with Proxima Centaurus, gaining speed rapidly. By the time he reaches his destination he will be traveling at faster-than-light-100. Icarus will be brought back to this universe within Centaurus itself. The explosion should destroy the star and wash away most of its planets—including their central hub-planet, Armun. There is no way they can halt Icarus, once he has been launched. No defense is possible. Nothing can stop him. It is a real fact."

"When will he be ready?"

Sherikov's eyes flickered. "Soon."

"Exactly how soon?"

The big Pole hesitated. "As a matter of fact, there's only one thing holding us back."

Sherikov led Reinhart around to the other side of the lab. He pushed a lab guard out of the way.

"See this?" He tapped a round globe, open at one end, the size of a grapefruit. "This is holding us up."

"What is it?"

"The central control turret. This thing brings Icarus back to sub-faster-than-light flight at the correct moment. It must be absolutely accurate. Icarus will be within the star only a matter of a microsecond. If the turret does not function exactly, Icarus will pass out the other side and shoot beyond the Centauran system."

"How near completed is this turret?"

Sherikov hedged uncertainly, spreading out his big hands. "Who can say? It must be wired with infinitely minute equipment—microscope grapples and wires invisible to the naked eye."

"Can you name any completion date?"

Sherikov reached into his coat and brought out a manila folder. "I've drawn up the data for the SRB machines, giving a date of completion. You can go ahead and feed it. I entered ten days as the maximum period. The machines can work from that."

Reinhart accepted the folder cautiously. "You're sure about the date? I'm not convinced I can trust you, Sherikov."

Sherikov's features darkened. "You'll have to take a chance, Commissioner. I don't trust you any more than you trust me. I know how much you'd like an excuse to get me out of here and one of your puppets in."

Reinhart studied the huge scientist thoughtfully. Sherikov was going to be a hard nut to crack. Designs was responsible to Security, not the Council. Sherikov was losing ground—but he was still a potential danger. Stubborn, individualistic, refusing to subordinate his welfare to the general good.

"All right." Reinhart put the folder slowly away in his coat. "I'll feed it. But you better be able to come through. There can't be any slip-ups. Too much hangs on the next few days."

"If the odds change in our favor are you going to give the mobilization order?"

"Yes," Reinhart stated. "I'll give the order the moment I see the odds change."

Standing in front of the machines, Reinhart waited nervously for the results. It was two o'clock in the afternoon. The day was warm, a pleasant May afternoon. Outside the building the daily life of the planet went on as usual.

As usual? Not exactly. The feeling was in the air, an expanding excitement growing every day. Terra had waited a long time. The attack on Proxima Centaurus had to come—and the sooner the better. The ancient Centauran Empire hemmed in Terra, bottled the human race up in its one system. A vast, suffocating net draped across the heavens, cutting Terra off from the bright diamonds beyond.... And it had to end.

The SRB machines whirred, the visible combination disappearing. For a time no ratio showed. Reinhart tensed, his body rigid. He waited.

The new ratio appeared.

Reinhart gasped. 7-6. Toward Terra!

Within five minutes the emergency mobilization alert had been flashed to all Government departments. The Council and President Duffe had been called to immediate session. Everything was happening fast.

But there was no doubt. 7-6. In Terra's favor. Reinhart hurried frantically to get his papers in order, in time for the Council session.

At histo-research the message plate was quickly pulled from the confidential slot and rushed across the central lab to the chief official.

"Look at this!" Fredman dropped the plate on his superior's desk. "Look at it!"

Harper picked up the plate, scanning it rapidly. "Sounds like the real thing. I didn't think we'd live to see it."

Fredman left the room, hurrying down the hall. He entered the time bubble office. "Where's the bubble?" he demanded, looking around.

One of the technicians looked slowly up. "Back about two hundred years. We're coming up with interesting data on the War of 1914. According to material the bubble has already brought up—"

"Cut it. We're through with routine work. Get the bubble back to the present. From now on all equipment has to be free for Military work."

"But—the bubble is regulated automatically."

"You can bring it back manually."

"It's risky." The technician hedged. "If the emergency requires it, I suppose we could take a chance and cut the automatic."

"The emergency requires *everything*," Fredman said feelingly.

"But the odds might change back," Margaret Duffe, President of the Council, said nervously. "Any minute they can revert."

"This is our chance!" Reinhart snapped, his temper rising. "What the hell's the matter with you? We've waited years for this."

The Council buzzed with excitement. Margaret Duffe hesitated uncertainly, her blue eyes clouded with worry. "I realize the opportunity is here. At least, statistically. But the new odds have just appeared. How do we know they'll last? They stand on the basis of a single weapon."

"You're wrong. You don't grasp the situation." Reinhart held himself in check with great effort. "Sherikov's weapon tipped the ratio in our favor. But the odds have been moving in our direction for months. It was only a question of time. The new balance was inevitable, sooner or later. It's not just Sherikov. He's only one factor in this. It's all nine planets of the Sol System—not a single man."

One of the Councilmen stood up. "The President must be aware the entire planet is eager to end this waiting. All our activities for the past eighty years have been directed toward—"

Reinhart moved close to the slender President of the Council. "If you don't approve the war, there probably will be mass rioting. Public reaction will be strong. Damn strong. And you know it."

Margaret Duffe shot him a cold glance. "You sent out the emergency order to force my hand. You were fully aware of what you were doing. You knew once the order was out there'd be no stopping things."

A murmur rushed through the Council, gaining volume. "We have to approve the war!... We're committed!... It's too late to turn back!"

Shouts, angry voices, insistent waves of sound lapped around Margaret Duffe. "I'm as much for the war as anybody," she said sharply. "I'm only urging moderation. An inter-system war is a big thing. We're going to war because a machine says we have a statistical chance of winning."

"There's no use starting the war unless we can win it," Reinhart said. "The SRB machines tell us whether we can win."

"They tell us our *chance* of winning. They don't guarantee anything."

"What more can we ask, beside a good chance of winning?"

Margaret Duffe clamped her jaw together tightly. "All right. I hear all the clamor. I won't stand in the way of Council approval. The vote can go ahead." Her cold, alert eyes appraised Reinhart. "Especially since the emergency order has already been sent out to all Government departments."

"Good." Reinhart stepped away with relief. "Then it's settled. We can finally go ahead with full mobilization."

Mobilization proceeded rapidly. The next forty-eight hours were alive with activity.

Reinhart attended a policy-level Military briefing in the Council rooms, conducted by Fleet Commander Carleton.

"You can see our strategy," Carleton said. He traced a diagram on the blackboard with a wave of his hand. "Sherikov states it'll take eight more days to complete the faster-than-light bomb. During that time the fleet we have near the Centauran system will take up positions. As the bomb goes off the fleet will begin operations against the remaining Centauran ships. Many will no doubt survive the blast, but with Armun gone we should be able to handle them."

Reinhart took Commander Carleton's place. "I can report on the economic situation. Every factory on Terra is converted to arms production. With Armun out of the way we should be able to promote mass insurrection among the Centauran colonies. An inter-system Empire is hard to maintain, even with ships that approach light speed. Local war-lords should pop up all over the place. We want to have weapons available for them and ships starting *now* to reach them in time. Eventually we hope to provide a unifying principle around which the colonies can all collect. Our interest is more economic than political. They can have any kind of government they want, as long as they act as supply areas for us. As our eight system planets act now."

Carleton resumed his report. "Once the Centauran fleet has been scattered we can begin the crucial stage of the war. The landing of men and supplies from the ships we have waiting in all key areas throughout the Centauran system. In this stage—"

Reinhart moved away. It was hard to believe only two days had passed since the mobilization order had been sent out. The whole system was alive, functioning with feverish activity. Countless problems were being solved—but much remained.

He entered the lift and ascended to the SRB room, curious to see if there had been any change in the machines' reading. He found it the same. So far so good. Did the Centaurans know about Icarus? No doubt; but there wasn't anything they could do about it. At least, not in eight days.

Kaplan came over to Reinhart, sorting a new batch of data that had come in. The lab organizer searched through his data. "An amusing item came in. It might interest you." He handed a message plate to Reinhart.

It was from histo-research:

May 9, 2136

This is to report that in bringing the research time bubble up to the present the manual return was used for the first time. Therefore a clean break was not made, and a quantity of material from the past was brought forward. This material included an individual from the early twentieth century who escaped from the lab immediately. He has not yet been taken into protective custody. Histo-research regrets this incident, but attributes it to the emergency.

E. Fredman

Reinhart handed the plate back to Kaplan. "Interesting. A man from the past—hauled into the middle of the biggest war the universe has seen."

"Strange things happen. I wonder what the machines will think."

"Hard to say. Probably nothing." Reinhart left the room and hurried along the corridor to his own office.

As soon as he was inside he called Sherikov on the vidscreen, using the confidential line.

The Pole's heavy features appeared. "Good day, Commissioner. How's the war effort?"

"Fine. How's the turret wiring proceeding?"

A faint frown flickered across Sherikov's face. "As a matter of fact, Commissioner—"

"What's the matter?" Reinhart said sharply.

Sherikov floundered. "You know how these things are. I've taken my crew off it and tried robot workers. They have greater dexterity, but they can't make decisions. This calls for more than mere dexterity. This calls for—" He searched for the word. "—for an *artist*."

Reinhart's face hardened. "Listen, Sherikov. You have eight days left to complete the bomb. The data given to the SRB machines contained that information. The 7-6 ratio is based on that estimate. If you don't come through—"

Sherikov twisted in embarrassment. "Don't get excited, Commissioner. We'll complete it."

"I hope so. Call me as soon as it's done." Reinhart snapped off the connection. If Sherikov let them down he'd have him taken out and shot. The whole war depended on the faster-than-light bomb.

The vidscreen glowed again. Reinhart snapped it on. Kaplan's face formed on it. The lab organizer's face was pale and frozen. "Commissioner, you better come up to the SRB office. Something's happened."

"What is it?"

"I'll show you."

Alarmed, Reinhart hurried out of his office and down the corridor. He found Kaplan standing in front of the SRB machines. "What's the story?" Reinhart demanded. He glanced down at the reading. It was unchanged.

Kaplan held up a message plate nervously. "A moment ago I fed this into the machines. After I saw the results I quickly removed it. It's that item I showed you. From histo-research. About the man from the past."

"What happened when you fed it?"

Kaplan swallowed unhappily. "I'll show you. I'll do it again. Exactly as before." He fed the plate into a moving intake belt. "Watch the visible figures," Kaplan muttered.

Reinhart watched, tense and rigid. For a moment nothing happened. 7-6 continued to show. Then...

The figures disappeared. The machines faltered. New figures showed briefly. 4-24 for Centaurus. Reinhart gasped, suddenly sick with apprehension. But the figures vanished. New figures appeared. 16-

38 for Centaurus. Then 48-86. 79-15 in Terra's favor. Then nothing. The machines whirred, but nothing happened.

Nothing at all. No figures. Only a blank.

"What's it mean?" Reinhart muttered, dazed.

"It's fantastic. We didn't think this could—"

"*What's happened?*"

"The machines aren't able to handle the item. No reading can come. It's data they can't integrate. They can't use it for prediction material, and it throws off all their other figures."

"Why?"

"It's—it's a variable." Kaplan was shaking, white-lipped and pale. "Something from which no inference can be made. The man from the past. The machines can't deal with him. The variable man!"

CHAPTER TWO

Thomas Cole was sharpening a knife with his whetstone when the tornado hit.

The knife belonged to the lady in the big green house. Every time Cole came by with his Fixit cart the lady had something to be sharpened. Once in awhile she gave him a cup of coffee, hot black coffee from an old bent pot. He liked that fine; he enjoyed good coffee.

The day was drizzly and overcast. Business had been bad. An automobile had scared his two horses. On bad days less people were outside and he had to get down from the cart and go to ring doorbells.

But the man in the yellow house had given him a dollar for fixing his electric refrigerator. Nobody else had been able to fix it, not even the factory man. The dollar would go a long way. A dollar was a lot.

He knew it was a tornado even before it hit him. Everything was silent. He was bent over his whetstone, the reins between his knees, absorbed in his work.

He had done a good job on the knife; he was almost finished. He spat on the blade and was holding it up to see—and then the tornado came.

All at once it was there, completely around him. Nothing but grayness. He and the cart and horses seemed to be in a calm spot in the center of the tornado. They were moving in a great silence, gray mist everywhere.

And while he was wondering what to do, and how to get the lady's knife back to her, all at once there was a bump and the tornado tipped him over, sprawled out on the ground. The horses screamed in fear, struggling to pick themselves up. Cole got quickly to his feet.

Where was he?

The grayness was gone. White walls stuck up on all sides. A deep light gleamed down, not daylight but something like it. The team was pulling the cart on its side, dragging it along, tools and equipment falling out. Cole righted the cart, leaping up onto the seat.

And for the first time saw the people.

Men, with astonished white faces, in some sort of uniforms. Shouts, noise and confusion. And a feeling of danger!

Cole headed the team toward the door. Hoofs thundered steel against steel as they pounded through the doorway, scattering the astonished men in all directions. He was out in a wide hall. A building, like a hospital.

The hall divided. More men were coming, spilling from all sides.

Shouting and milling in excitement, like white ants. Something cut past him, a beam of dark violet. It seared off a corner of the cart, leaving the wood smoking.

Cole felt fear. He kicked at the terrified horses. They reached a big door, crashing wildly against it. The door gave—and they were outside, bright sunlight blinking down on them. For a sickening second the cart tilted, almost turning over. Then the horses gained speed, racing across an open field, toward a distant line of green, Cole holding tightly to the reins.

Behind him the little white-faced men had come out and were standing in a group, gesturing frantically. He could hear their faint shrill shouts.

But he had got away. He was safe. He slowed the horses down and began to breathe again.

The woods were artificial. Some kind of park. But the park was wild and overgrown. A dense jungle of twisted plants. Everything growing in confusion.

The park was empty. No one was there. By the position of the sun he could tell it was either early morning or late afternoon. The smell of the flowers and grass, the dampness of the leaves, indicated morning. It had been late afternoon when the tornado had picked him up. And the sky had been overcast and cloudy.

Cole considered. Clearly, he had been carried a long way. The hospital, the men with white faces, the odd lighting, the accented words he had caught—everything indicated he was no longer in Nebraska—maybe not even in the United States.

Some of his tools had fallen out and gotten lost along the way. Cole collected everything that remained, sorting them, running his fingers over each tool with affection. Some of the little chisels and wood gouges were gone. The bit box had opened, and most of the smaller bits had been lost. He gathered up those that remained and replaced them tenderly in the box. He took a key-hole saw down, and with an oil rag wiped it carefully and replaced it.

Above the cart the sun rose slowly in the sky. Cole peered up, his horny hand over his eyes. A big man, stoop-shouldered, his chin gray and stubbled. His clothes wrinkled and dirty. But his eyes were clear, a pale blue, and his hands were finely made.

He could not stay in the park. They had seen him ride that way; they would be looking for him.

Far above something shot rapidly across the sky. A tiny black dot moving with incredible haste. A second dot followed. The two dots were gone almost before he saw them. They were utterly silent.

Cole frowned, perturbed. The dots made him uneasy. He would have to keep moving—and looking for food. His stomach was already beginning to rumble and groan.

Work. There was plenty he could do: gardening, sharpening, grinding, repair work on machines and clocks, fixing all kinds of household things. Even painting and odd jobs and carpentry and chores.

He could do anything. Anything people wanted done. For a meal and pocket money.

Thomas Cole urged the team into life, moving forward. He sat hunched over in the seat, watching intently, as the Fixit cart rolled slowly across the tangled grass, through the jungle of trees and flowers.

Reinhart hurried, racing his cruiser at top speed, followed by a second ship, a military escort. The ground sped by below him, a blur of gray and green.

The remains of New York lay spread out, a twisted, blunted ruin overgrown with weeds and grass. The great atomic wars of the twentieth century had turned virtually the whole seaboard area into an endless waste of slag.

Slag and weeds below him. And then the sudden tangle that had been Central Park.

Histo-research came into sight. Reinhart swooped down, bringing his cruiser to rest at the small supply field behind the main buildings.

Harper, the chief official of the department, came quickly over as soon as Reinhart's ship landed.

"Frankly, we don't understand why you consider this matter important," Harper said uneasily.

Reinhart shot him a cold glance. "I'll be the judge of what's important. Are you the one who gave the order to bring the bubble back manually?"

"Fredman gave the actual order. In line with your directive to have all facilities ready for—"

Reinhart headed toward the entrance of the research building. "Where is Fredman?"

"Inside."

"I want to see him. Let's go."

Fredman met them inside. He greeted Reinhart calmly, showing no emotion. "Sorry to cause you trouble, Commissioner. We were trying to get the station in order for the war. We wanted the bubble back as quickly as possible." He eyed Reinhart curiously. "No doubt the man and his cart will soon be picked up by your police."

"I want to know everything that happened, in exact detail."

Fredman shifted uncomfortably. "There's not much to tell. I gave the order to have the automatic setting canceled and the bubble brought back manually. At the moment the signal reached it, the bubble was passing through the spring of 1913. As it broke loose, it tore off a piece of ground on which this person and his cart were located. The person naturally was brought up to the present, inside the bubble."

"Didn't any of your instruments tell you the bubble was loaded?"

"We were too excited to take any readings. Half an hour after the manual control was thrown, the bubble materialized in the observation room. It was de-energized before anyone noticed what was inside. We tried to stop him but he drove the cart out into the hall, bowling us out of the way. The horses were in a panic."

"What kind of cart was it?"

"There was some kind of sign on it. Painted in black letters on both sides. No one saw what it was."

"Go ahead. What happened then?"

"Somebody fired a Slem-ray after him, but it missed. The horses carried him out of the building and onto the grounds. By the time we reached the exit the cart was half way to the park."

Reinhart reflected. "If he's still in the park we should have him shortly. But we must be careful." He was already starting back toward his ship, leaving Fredman behind. Harper fell in beside him.

Reinhart halted by his ship. He beckoned some Government guards over. "Put the executive staff of this department under arrest. I'll have them tried on a treason count, later on." He smiled ironically as Harper's face blanched sickly pale. "There's a war going on. You'll be lucky if you get off alive."

Reinhart entered his ship and left the surface, rising rapidly into the sky. A second ship followed after him, a military escort. Reinhart flew high above the sea of gray slag, the unrecovered waste area. He passed over a sudden square of green set in the ocean of gray. Reinhart gazed back at it until it was gone.

Central Park. He could see police ships racing through the sky, ships and transports loaded with troops, heading toward the square of green. On the ground some heavy guns and surface cars rumbled along, lines of black approaching the park from all sides.

They would have the man soon. But meanwhile, the SRB machines were blank. And on the SRB machines' readings the whole war depended.

About noon the cart reached the edge of the park. Cole rested for a moment, allowing the horses time to crop at the thick grass. The silent expanse of slag amazed him. What had happened? Nothing stirred. No buildings, no sign of life. Grass and weeds poked up occasionally through it, breaking the flat surface here and there, but even so, the sight gave him an uneasy chill.

Cole drove the cart slowly out onto the slag, studying the sky above him. There was nothing to hide him, now that he was out of the park. The slag was bare and uniform, like the ocean. If he were spotted…

A horde of tiny black dots raced across the sky, coming rapidly closer. Presently they veered to the right and disappeared. More planes, wingless metal planes. He watched them go, driving slowly on.

Half an hour later something appeared ahead. Cole slowed the cart down, peering to see. The slag came to an end. He had reached its limits. Ground appeared, dark soil and grass. Weeds grew everywhere. Ahead of him, beyond the end of the slag, was a line of buildings, houses of some sort. Or sheds.

Houses, probably. But not like any he had ever seen.

The houses were uniform, all exactly the same. Like little green shells, rows of them, several hundred. There was a little lawn in front of each. Lawn, a path, a front porch, bushes in a meager row around each house. But the houses were all alike and very small.

Little green shells in precise, even rows. He urged the cart cautiously forward, toward the houses.

No one seemed to be around. He entered a street between two rows of houses, the hoofs of his two horses sounding loudly in the silence. He was in some kind of town. But there were no dogs or children. Everything was neat and silent. Like a model. An exhibit. It made him uncomfortable.

A young man walking along the pavement gaped at him in wonder. An oddly-dressed youth, in a toga-like cloak that hung down to his knees. A single piece of fabric. And sandals.

Or what looked like sandals. Both the cloak and the sandals were of some strange half-luminous material. It glowed faintly in the sunlight. Metallic, rather than cloth.

A woman was watering flowers at the edge of a lawn. She straightened up as his team of horses came near. Her eyes widened in astonishment—and then fear. Her mouth fell open in a soundless O and her sprinkling can slipped from her fingers and rolled silently onto the lawn.

Cole blushed and turned his head quickly away. The woman was scarcely dressed! He flicked the reins and urged the horses to hurry.

Behind him, the woman still stood. He stole a brief, hasty look back—and then shouted hoarsely to his team, ears scarlet. He had seen right. She wore only a pair of translucent shorts. Nothing else. A mere fragment of the same half-luminous material that glowed and sparkled. The rest of her small body was utterly naked.

He slowed the team down. She had been pretty. Brown hair and eyes, deep red lips. Quite a good figure. Slender waist, downy legs, bare and supple, full breasts. He clamped the thought furiously off. He had to get to work. Business.

Cole halted the Fixit cart and leaped down onto the pavement. He selected a house at random and approached it cautiously. The house was attractive. It had a certain simple beauty. But it looked frail—and exactly like the others.

He stepped up on the porch. There was no bell. He searched for it, running his hand uneasily over the surface of the door. All at once there was a click, a sharp snap on a level with his eyes. Cole glanced up, startled. A lens was vanishing as the door section slid over it. He had been photographed.

While he was wondering what it meant, the door swung suddenly open. A man filled up the entrance, a big man in a tan uniform, blocking the way ominously.

"What do you want?" the man demanded.

"I'm looking for work," Cole murmured. "Any kind of work. I can do anything, fix any kind of thing. I repair broken objects. Things that need mending." His voice trailed off uncertainly. "Anything at all."

"Apply to the Placement Department of the Federal Activities Control Board," the man said crisply. "You know all occupational therapy is handled through them." He eyed Cole curiously. "Why have you got on those ancient clothes?"

"Ancient? Why, I—"

The man gazed past him at the Fixit cart and the two dozing horses. "What's that? What are those two animals? *Horses?*" The man rubbed his jaw, studying Cole intently. "That's strange," he said.

"Strange?" Cole murmured uneasily. "Why?"

"There haven't been any horses for over a century. All the horses were wiped out during the Fifth Atomic War. That's why it's strange."

Cole tensed, suddenly alert. There was something in the man's eyes, a hardness, a piercing look. Cole moved back off the porch, onto the path. He had to be careful. Something was wrong.

"I'll be going," he murmured.

"There haven't been any horses for over a hundred years." The man came toward Cole. "Who are you? Why are you dressed up like that? Where did you get that vehicle and pair of horses?"

"I'll be going," Cole repeated, moving away.

The man whipped something from his belt, a thin metal tube. He stuck it toward Cole.

It was a rolled-up paper, a thin sheet of metal in the form of a tube. Words, some kind of script. He could not make any of them out. The man's picture, rows of numbers, figures...

"I'm Director Winslow," the man said. "Federal Stockpile Conservation. You better talk fast, or there'll be a Security car here in five minutes."

Cole moved—fast. He raced, head down, back along the path to the cart, toward the street.

Something hit him. A wall of force, throwing him down on his face. He sprawled in a heap, numb and dazed. His body ached, vibrating wildly, out of control. Waves of shock rolled over him, gradually diminishing.

He got shakily to his feet. His head spun. He was weak, shattered, trembling violently. The man was coming down the walk after him. Cole pulled himself onto the cart, gasping and retching. The horses jumped into life. Cole rolled over against the seat, sick with the motion of the swaying cart.

He caught hold of the reins and managed to drag himself up in a sitting position. The cart gained speed, turning a corner. Houses flew past. Cole urged the team weakly, drawing great shuddering breaths. Houses and streets, a blur of motion, as the cart flew faster and faster along.

Then he was leaving the town, leaving the neat little houses behind. He was on some sort of highway. Big buildings, factories, on both sides of the highway. Figures, men watching in astonishment.

After awhile the factories fell behind. Cole slowed the team down. What had the man meant? Fifth Atomic War. Horses destroyed. It didn't make sense. And they had things he knew nothing about. Force fields. Planes without wings—soundless.

Cole reached around in his pockets. He found the identification tube the man had handed him. In the excitement he had carried it off. He unrolled the tube slowly and began to study it. The writing was strange to him.

For a long time he studied the tube. Then, gradually, he became aware of something. Something in the top right-hand corner.

A date. October 6, 2128.

Cole's vision blurred. Everything spun and wavered around him. October, 2128. Could it be?

But he held the paper in his hand. Thin, metal paper. Like foil. And it had to be. It said so, right in the corner, printed on the paper itself.

Cole rolled the tube up slowly, numbed with shock. Two hundred years. It didn't seem possible. But things were beginning to make sense. He was in the future, two hundred years in the future.

While he was mulling this over, the swift black Security ship appeared overhead, diving rapidly toward the horse-drawn cart, as it moved slowly along the road.

Reinhart's vidscreen buzzed. He snapped it quickly on. "Yes?"

"Report from Security."

"Put it through." Reinhart waited tensely as the lines locked in place. The screen re-lit.

"This is Dixon. Western Regional Command." The officer cleared his throat, shuffling his message plates. "The man from the past has been reported, moving away from the New York area."

"Which side of your net?"

"Outside. He evaded the net around Central Park by entering one of the small towns at the rim of the slag area."

"*Evaded?*"

"We assumed he would avoid the towns. Naturally the net failed to encompass any of the towns."

Reinhart's jaw stiffened. "Go on."

"He entered the town of Petersville a few minutes before the net closed around the park. We burned the park level, but naturally found nothing. He had already gone. An hour later we received a report from a resident in Petersville, an official of the Stockpile Conservation Department. The man from the past had come to his door, looking for work. Winslow, the official, engaged him in conversation, trying to hold onto him, but he escaped, driving his cart off. Winslow called Security right away, but by then it was too late."

"Report to me as soon as anything more comes in. We must have him—and damn soon." Reinhart snapped the screen off. It died quickly.

He sat back in his chair, waiting.

Cole saw the shadow of the Security ship. He reacted at once. A second after the shadow passed over him, Cole was out of the cart, running and falling. He rolled, twisting and turning, pulling his body as far away from the cart as possible.

There was a blinding roar and flash of white light. A hot wind rolled over Cole, picking him up and tossing him like a leaf. He shut his eyes, letting his body relax. He bounced, falling and striking the ground. Gravel and stones tore into his face, his knees, the palms of his hands.

Cole cried out, shrieking in pain. His body was on fire. He was being consumed, incinerated by the blinding white orb of fire. The orb expanded, growing in size, swelling like some monstrous sun, twisted and bloated. The end had come. There was no hope. He gritted his teeth…

The greedy orb faded, dying down. It sputtered and winked out, blackening into ash. The air reeked, a bitter acrid smell. His clothes were burning and smoking. The ground under him was hot, baked dry, seared by the blast. But he was alive. At least, for awhile.

Cole opened his eyes slowly. The cart was gone. A great hole gaped where it had been, a shattered sore in the center of the highway. An ugly cloud hung above the hole, black and ominous. Far above, the wingless plane circled, watching for any signs of life.

Cole lay, breathing shallowly, slowly. Time passed. The sun moved across the sky with agonizing slowness. It was perhaps four in the afternoon. Cole calculated mentally. In three hours it would be dark. If he could stay alive until then...

Had the plane seen him leap from the cart?

He lay without moving. The late afternoon sun beat down on him. He felt sick, nauseated and feverish. His mouth was dry.

Some ants ran over his outstretched hand. Gradually, the immense black cloud was beginning to drift away, dispersing into a formless blob.

The cart was gone. The thought lashed against him, pounding at his brain, mixing with his labored pulse-beat. *Gone.* Destroyed. Nothing but ashes and debris remained. The realization dazed him.

Finally the plane finished its circling, winging its way toward the horizon. At last it vanished. The sky was clear.

Cole got unsteadily to his feet. He wiped his face shakily. His body ached and trembled. He spat a couple times, trying to clear his mouth. The plane would probably send in a report. People would be coming to look for him. Where could he go?

To his right a line of hills rose up, a distant green mass. Maybe he could reach them. He began to walk slowly. He had to be very careful. They were looking for him—and they had weapons. Incredible weapons.

He would be lucky to still be alive when the sun set. His team and Fixit cart were gone—and all his tools. Cole reached into his pockets, searching through them hopefully. He brought out some small screwdrivers, a little pair of cutting pliers, some wire, some solder, the whetstone, and finally the lady's knife.

Only a few small tools remained. He had lost everything else. But without the cart he was safer, harder to spot. They would have more trouble finding him, on foot.

Cole hurried along, crossing the level fields toward the distant range of hills.

The call came through to Reinhart almost at once. Dixon's features formed on the vidscreen. "I have a further report, Commissioner." Dixon scanned the plate. "Good news. The man from the past was sighted moving away from Petersville, along highway 13, at about ten miles an hour, on his horse-drawn cart. Our ship bombed him immediately."

"Did—did you get him?"

"The pilot reports no sign of life after the blast."

Reinhart's pulse almost stopped. He sank back in his chair. "Then he's dead!"

"Actually, we won't know for certain until we can examine the debris. A surface car is speeding toward the spot. We should have the complete report in a short time.   We'll notify you as soon as the information comes in."

Reinhart reached out and cut the screen. It faded into darkness. Had they got the man from the past? Or had he escaped again? Weren't they ever going to get him? Couldn't he be captured? And meanwhile, the SRB machines were silent, showing nothing at all.

Reinhart sat brooding, waiting impatiently for the report of the surface car to come in.

It was evening.

"Come on!" Steven shouted, running frantically after his brother. "Come on back!"

"Catch me." Earl ran and ran, down the side of the hill, over behind a military storage depot, along a neotex fence, jumping finally down into Mrs. Norris' back yard.

Steven hurried after his brother, sobbing for breath, shouting and gasping as he ran. "Come back! You come back with that!"

"What's he got?" Sally Tate demanded, stepping out suddenly to block Steven's way.

Steven halted, his chest rising and falling. "He's got my intersystem vidsender." His small face twisted with rage and misery. "He better give it back!"

Earl came circling around from the right. In the warm gloom of evening he was almost invisible. "Here I am," he announced. "What you going to do?"

Steven glared at him hotly. His eyes made out the square box in Earl's hands. "You give that back! Or—or I'll tell Dad."

Earl laughed. "Make me."

"Dad'll make you."

"You better give it to him," Sally said.

"Catch me." Earl started off. Steven pushed Sally out of the way, lashing wildly at his brother. He collided with him, throwing him sprawling. The box fell from Earl's hands. It skidded to the pavement, crashing into the side of a guide-light post.

Earl and Steven picked themselves up slowly. They gazed down at the broken box.

"See?" Steven shrilled, tears filling his eyes. "See what you did?"

"You did it. You pushed into me."

"You did it!" Steven bent down and picked up the box. He carried it over to the guide-light, sitting down on the curb to examine it.

Earl came slowly over. "If you hadn't pushed me it wouldn't have got broken."

Night was descending rapidly. The line of hills rising above the town were already lost in darkness. A few lights had come on here and there. The evening was warm. A surface car slammed its doors, some place off in the distance. In the sky ships droned back and forth, weary commuters coming home from work in the big underground factory units.

Thomas Cole came slowly toward the three children grouped around the guide-light. He moved with difficulty, his body sore and bent with fatigue. Night had come, but he was not safe yet.

He was tired, exhausted and hungry. He had walked a long way. And he had to have something to eat—soon.

A few feet from the children Cole stopped. They were all intent and absorbed by the box on Steven's knees. Suddenly a hush fell over the children. Earl looked up slowly.

In the dim light the big stooped figure of Thomas Cole seemed extra menacing. His long arms hung down loosely at his sides. His face was lost in shadow. His body was shapeless, indistinct. A big unformed statue, standing silently a few feet away, unmoving in the half-darkness.

"Who are you?" Earl demanded, his voice low.

"What do you want?" Sally said. The children edged away nervously. "Get away."

Cole came toward them. He bent down a little. The beam from the guide-light crossed his features. Lean, prominent nose, beak-like, faded blue eyes…

Steven scrambled to his feet, clutching the vidsender box. "You get out of here!"

"Wait." Cole smiled crookedly at them. His voice was dry and raspy. "What do you have there?" He pointed with his long, slender fingers. "The box you're holding."

The children were silent. Finally Steven stirred. "It's my inter-system vidsender."

"Only it doesn't work," Sally said.

"Earl broke it." Steven glared at his brother bitterly. "Earl threw it down and broke it."

Cole smiled a little. He sank down wearily on the edge of the curb, sighing with relief. He had been walking too long. His body ached with fatigue. He was hungry, and tired. For a long time he sat, wiping perspiration from his neck and face, too exhausted to speak.

"Who are you?" Sally demanded, at last. "Why do you have on those funny clothes? Where did you come from?"

"Where?" Cole looked around at the children. "From a long way off. A long way." He shook his head slowly from side to side, trying to clear it.

"What's your therapy?" Earl said.

"My therapy?"

"What do you do? Where do you work?"

Cole took a deep breath and let it out again slowly. "I fix things. All kinds of things. Any kind."

Earl sneered. "Nobody fixes things. When they break you throw them away."

Cole didn't hear him. Sudden need had roused him, getting him suddenly to his feet. "You know any work I can find?" he demanded. "Things I could do? I can fix anything. Clocks, type-writers, refrigerators, pots and pans. Leaks in the roof. I can fix anything there is."

Steven held out his inter-system vidsender. "Fix this."

There was silence. Slowly, Cole's eyes focused on the box. "That?"

"My sender. Earl broke it."

Cole took the box slowly. He turned it over, holding it up to the light. He frowned, concentrating on it. His long, slender fingers moved carefully over the surface, exploring it.

"He'll steal it!" Earl said suddenly.

"No." Cole shook his head vaguely. "I'm reliable." His sensitive fingers found the studs that held the box together. He depressed the studs, pushing them expertly in. The box opened, revealing its complex interior.

"He got it open," Sally whispered.

"Give it back!" Steven demanded, a little frightened. He held out his hand. "I want it back."

The three children watched Cole apprehensively. Cole fumbled in his pocket. Slowly he brought out his tiny screwdrivers and pliers. He laid them in a row beside him. He made no move to return the box.

"I want it back," Steven said feebly.

Cole looked up. His faded blue eyes took in the sight of the three children standing before him in the gloom. "I'll fix it for you. You said you wanted it fixed."

"I want it back." Steven stood on one foot, then the other, torn by doubt and indecision. "Can you really fix it? Can you make it work again?"

"Yes."

"All right. Fix it for me, then."

A sly smile flickered across Cole's tired face. "Now, wait a minute. If I fix it, will you bring me something to eat? I'm not fixing it for nothing."

"Something to eat?"

"Food. I need hot food. Maybe some coffee."

Steven nodded. "Yes. I'll get it for you."

Cole relaxed. "Fine. That's fine." He turned his attention back to the box resting between his knees. "Then I'll fix it for you. I'll fix it for you good."

His fingers flew, working and twisting, tracing down wires and relays, exploring and examining. Finding out about the inter-system vidsender. Discovering how it worked.

Steven slipped into the house through the emergency door. He made his way to the kitchen with great care, walking on tip-toe. He punched the kitchen controls at random, his heart beating excitedly. The stove began to whirr, purring into life. Meter readings came on, crossing toward the completion marks.

Presently the stove opened, sliding out a tray of steaming dishes. The mechanism clicked off, dying into silence. Steven grabbed up the contents of the tray, filling his arms. He carried everything down the hall, out the emergency door and into the yard. The yard was dark. Steven felt his way carefully along.

He managed to reach the guide-light without dropping anything at all.

Thomas Cole got slowly to his feet as Steven came into view. "Here," Steven said. He dumped the food onto the curb, gasping for breath. "Here's the food. Is it finished?"

Cole held out the inter-system vidsender. "It's finished. It was pretty badly smashed."

Earl and Sally gazed up, wide-eyed. "Does it work?" Sally asked.

"Of course not," Earl stated. "How could it work? He couldn't—"

"Turn it on!" Sally nudged Steven eagerly. "See if it works."

Steven was holding the box under the light, examining the switches. He clicked the main switch on. The indicator light gleamed. "It lights up," Steven said.

"Say something into it."

Steven spoke into the box. "Hello! Hello! This is operator 6-Z75 calling. Can you hear me? This is operator 6-Z75. Can you hear me?"

In the darkness, away from the beam of the guide-light, Thomas Cole sat crouched over the food. He ate gratefully, silently. It was good food, well cooked and seasoned. He drank a container of orange juice and then a sweet drink he didn't recognize. Most of the food was strange to him, but he didn't care. He had walked a long way and he was plenty hungry. And he still had a long way to go, before morning. He had to be deep in the hills before the sun came up. Instinct told him that he would be safe among the trees and tangled growth—at least, as safe as he could hope for.

He ate rapidly, intent on the food. He did not look up until he was finished. Then he got slowly to his feet, wiping his mouth with the back of his hand.

The three children were standing around in a circle, operating the inter-system vidsender. He watched them for a few minutes. None of them looked up from the small box. They were intent, absorbed in what they were doing.

"Well?" Cole said, at last. "Does it work all right?"

After a moment Steven looked up at him. There was a strange expression on his face. He nodded slowly. "Yes. Yes, it works. It works fine."

Cole grunted. "All right." He turned and moved away from the light. "That's fine."

The children watched silently until the figure of Thomas Cole had completely disappeared. Slowly, they turned and looked at each other. Then down at the box in Steven's hands. They gazed at the box in growing awe. Awe mixed with dawning fear.

Steven turned and edged toward his house. "I've got to show it to my Dad," he murmured, dazed. "He's got to know. *Somebody's* got to know!"

CHAPTER THREE

Eric Reinhart examined the vidsender box carefully, turning it around and around.

"Then he did escape from the blast," Dixon admitted reluctantly. "He must have leaped from the cart just before the concussion."

Reinhart nodded. "He escaped. He got away from you—twice." He pushed the vidsender box away and leaned abruptly toward the man standing uneasily in front of his desk. "What's your name again?"

"Elliot. Richard Elliot."

"And your son's name?"

"Steven."

"It was last night this happened?"

"About eight o'clock."

"Go on."

"Steven came into the house. He acted queerly. He was carrying his inter-system vidsender." Elliot pointed at the box on Reinhart's desk. "That. He was nervous and excited. I asked what was wrong. For awhile he couldn't tell me. He was quite upset. Then he showed me the vidsender." Elliot took a deep, shaky breath. "I could see right away it was different. You see I'm an electrical engineer. I had opened it once before, to put in a new battery. I had a fairly good idea how it should look." Elliot hesitated.

"Commissioner, it had been *changed*. A lot of the wiring was different. Moved around. Relays connected differently. Some parts were missing. New parts had been jury rigged out of old. Then I discovered the thing that made me call Security. The vidsender—it really *worked*."

"Worked?"

"You see, it never was anything more than a toy. With a range of a few city blocks. So the kids could call back and forth from their rooms. Like a sort of portable vidscreen. Commissioner, I tried out the vidsender, pushing the call button and speaking into the microphone. I—I got a ship of the line. A battleship, operating beyond Proxima Centaurus— over eight light years away. As far out as the actual vidsenders operate. Then I called Security. Right away."

For a time Reinhart was silent. Finally he tapped the box lying on the desk. "You got a ship of the line—with *this?*"

"That's right."

"How big are the regular vidsenders?"

Dixon supplied the information. "As big as a twenty-ton safe."

"That's what I thought." Reinhart waved his hand impatiently. "All right, Elliot. Thanks for turning the information over to us. That's all."

Security police led Elliot outside the office.

Reinhart and Dixon looked at each other. "This is bad," Reinhart said harshly. "He has some ability, some kind of mechanical ability. Genius, perhaps, to do a thing like this. Look at the period he came from, Dixon. The early part of the twentieth century. Before the wars began. That was a unique period. There was a certain vitality, a certain ability. It was a period of incredible growth and discovery. Edison. Pasteur. Burbank. The Wright brothers. Inventions and machines. People had an uncanny ability with machines. A kind of intuition about machines—which we don't have."

"You mean—"

"I mean a person like this coming into our own time is bad in itself, war or no war. He's too different. He's oriented along different lines. He has abilities we lack. This fixing skill of his. It throws us off, out of kilter. And with the war…

"Now I'm beginning to understand why the SRB machines couldn't factor him. It's impossible for us to understand this kind of person. Winslow says he asked for work, any kind of work. The man said he could do anything, fix anything. Do you understand what that means?"

"No," Dixon said. "What does it mean?"

"Can any of us fix anything? No. None of us can do that. We're specialized. Each of us has his own line, his own work. I understand my work, you understand yours. The tendency in evolution is toward greater and greater specialization. Man's society is an ecology that forces adaptation to it. Continual complexity makes it impossible for any of us to know anything outside our own personal field—I can't follow the work of the man sitting at the next desk over from me. Too much knowledge has piled up in each field. And there's too many fields.

"This man is different. He can fix anything, do anything. He doesn't work with knowledge, with science—the classified accumulation of facts. He *knows* nothing. It's not in his head, a form of learning. He works by intuition—his power is in his hands, not his head. Jack-of-all-trades. His hands! Like a painter, an artist. In his hands—and he cuts across our lives like a knife-blade."

"And the other problem?"

"The other problem is that this man, this variable man, has escaped into the Albertine Mountain range. Now we'll have one hell of a time finding him. He's clever—in a strange kind of way. Like some sort of animal. He's going to be hard to catch."

Reinhart sent Dixon out. After a moment he gathered up the handful of reports on his desk and carried them up to the SRB room. The SRB room was closed up, sealed off by a ring of armed Security police. Standing angrily before the ring of police was Peter Sherikov, his beard waggling angrily, his immense hands on his hips.

"What's going on?" Sherikov demanded. "Why can't I go in and peep at the odds?"

"Sorry." Reinhart cleared the police aside. "Come inside with me. I'll explain." The doors opened for them and they entered. Behind them the doors shut and the ring of police formed outside. "What brings you away from your lab?" Reinhart asked.

Sherikov shrugged. "Several things. I wanted to see you. I called you on the vidphone and they said you weren't available. I thought maybe something had happened. What's up?"

"I'll tell you in a few minutes." Reinhart called Kaplan over. "Here are some new items. Feed them in right away. I want to see if the machines can total them."

"Certainly, Commissioner." Kaplan took the message plates and placed them on an intake belt. The machines hummed into life.

"We'll know soon," Reinhart said, half aloud.

Sherikov shot him a keen glance. "We'll know what? Let me in on it. What's taking place?"

"We're in trouble. For twenty-four hours the machines haven't given any reading at all. Nothing but a blank. A total blank."

Sherikov's features registered disbelief. "But that isn't possible. *Some* odds exist at all times."

"The odds exist, but the machines aren't able to calculate them."

"Why not?"

"Because a variable factor has been introduced. A factor which the machines can't handle. They can't make any predictions from it."

"Can't they reject it?" Sherikov said slyly. "Can't they just—just *ignore* it?"

"No. It exists, as real data. Therefore it affects the balance of the material, the sum total of all other available data. To reject it would be to give a false reading. The machines can't reject any data that's known to be true."

Sherikov pulled moodily at his black beard. "I would be interested in knowing what sort of factor the machines can't handle. I thought they could take in all data pertaining to contemporary reality."

"They can. This factor has nothing to do with contemporary reality. That's the trouble. Histo-research in bringing its time bubble back from the past got overzealous and cut the circuit too quickly. The bubble came back loaded—with a man from the twentieth century. A man from the past."

"I see. A man from two centuries ago." The big Pole frowned. "And with a radically different Weltanschauung. No connection with our present society. Not integrated along our lines at all. Therefore the SRB machines are perplexed."

Reinhart grinned. "Perplexed? I suppose so. In any case, they can't do anything with the data about this man. The variable man. No statistics at all have been thrown up—no predictions have been made. And it knocks everything else out of phase. We're dependent on the constant showing of these odds. The whole war effort is geared around them."

"The horse-shoe nail. Remember the old poem? 'For want of a nail the shoe was lost. For want of the shoe the horse was lost. For want of the horse the rider was lost. For want—' "

"Exactly. A single factor coming along like this, one single individual, can throw everything off. It doesn't seem possible that one person could knock an entire society out of balance—but apparently it is."

"What are you doing about this man?"

"The Security police are organized in a mass search for him."

"Results?"

"He escaped into the Albertine Mountain Range last night. It'll be hard to find him. We must expect him to be loose for another forty-eight hours. It'll take that long for us to arrange the annihilation of the range area. Perhaps a trifle longer. And meanwhile—"

"Ready, Commissioner," Kaplan interrupted. "The new totals."

The SRB machines had finished factoring the new data. Reinhart and Sherikov hurried to take their places before the view windows.

For a moment nothing happened. Then odds were put up, locking in place.

Sherikov gasped. 99-2. In favor of Terra. "That's wonderful! Now we—"

The odds vanished. New odds took their places. 97-4. In favor of Centaurus. Sherikov groaned in astonished dismay. "Wait," Reinhart said to him. "I don't think they'll last."

The odds vanished. A rapid series of odds shot across the screen, a violent stream of numbers, changing almost instantly. At last the machines became silent.

Nothing showed. No odds. No totals at all. The view windows were blank.

"You see?" Reinhart murmured. "The same damn thing!"

Sherikov pondered. "Reinhart, you're too Anglo-Saxon, too impulsive. Be more Slavic. This man will be captured and destroyed within two days. You said so yourself. Meanwhile, we're all working night and day on the war effort. The war fleet is waiting near Proxima, taking up positions for the attack on the Centaurans. All our war plants are going full blast. By the time the attack date comes we'll have a full-sized invasion army ready to take off for the long trip to the Centauran colonies. The whole Terran population has been mobilized. The eight supply planets are pouring in material. All this is going on day and night, even without odds showing. Long before the attack comes this man will certainly be dead, and the machines will be able to show odds again."

Reinhart considered. "But it worries me, a man like that out in the open. Loose. A man who can't be predicted. It goes against science. We've been making statistical reports on society for two centuries. We have immense files of data. The machines are able to predict what each person and group will do at a given time, in a given situation. But this man is beyond all prediction. He's a variable. It's contrary to science."

"The indeterminate particle."

"What's that?"

"The particle that moves in such a way that we can't predict what position it will occupy at a given second. Random. The random particle."

"Exactly. It's—it's *unnatural.*"

Sherikov laughed sarcastically. "Don't worry about it, Commissioner. The man will be captured and things will return to their natural state. You'll be able to predict people again, like laboratory rats in a maze. By the way—why is this room guarded?"

"I don't want anyone to know the machines show no totals. It's dangerous to the war effort."

"Margaret Duffe, for example?"

Reinhart nodded reluctantly. "They're too timid, these parliamentarians. If they discover we have no SRB odds they'll want to shut down the war planning and go back to waiting."

"Too slow for you, Commissioner? Laws, debates, council meetings, discussions…. Saves a lot of time if one man has all the power. One man to tell people what to do, think for them, lead them around."

Reinhart eyed the big Pole critically. "That reminds me. How is Icarus coming? Have you continued to make progress on the control turret?"

A scowl crossed Sherikov's broad features. "The control turret?" He waved his big hand vaguely. "I would say it's coming along all right. We'll catch up in time."

Instantly Reinhart became alert. "Catch up? You mean you're still behind?"

"Somewhat. A little. But we'll catch up." Sherikov retreated toward the door. "Let's go down to the cafeteria and have a cup of coffee. You worry too much, Commissioner. Take things more in your stride."

"I suppose you're right." The two men walked out into the hall. "I'm on edge. This variable man. I can't get him out of my mind."

"Has he done anything yet?"

"Nothing important. Rewired a child's toy. A toy vidsender."

"Oh?" Sherikov showed interest. "What do you mean? What did he do?"

"I'll show you." Reinhart led Sherikov down the hall to his office. They entered and Reinhart locked the door. He handed Sherikov the toy and roughed in what Cole had done. A strange look crossed Sherikov's face. He found the studs on the box and depressed them. The box opened. The big Pole sat down at the desk and began to study the interior of the box. "You're sure it was the man from the past who rewired this?"

"Of course. On the spot. The boy damaged it playing. The variable man came along and the boy asked him to fix it. He fixed it, all right."

"Incredible." Sherikov's eyes were only an inch from the wiring. "Such tiny relays. How could he—"

"What?"

"Nothing." Sherikov got abruptly to his feet, closing the box carefully. "Can I take this along? To my lab? I'd like to analyze it more fully."

"Of course. But why?"

"No special reason. Let's go get our coffee." Sherikov headed toward the door. "You say you expect to capture this man in a day or so?"

"*Kill* him, not capture him. We've got to eliminate him as a piece of data. We're assembling the attack formations right now. No slip-ups, this time. We're in the process of setting up a cross-bombing pattern to level the entire Albertine range. He must be destroyed, within the next forty-eight hours."

Sherikov nodded absently. "Of course," he murmured. A preoccupied expression still remained on his broad features. "I understand perfectly."

Thomas Cole crouched over the fire he had built, warming his hands. It was almost morning. The sky was turning violet gray. The mountain air was crisp and chill. Cole shivered and pulled himself closer to the fire.

The heat felt good against his hands. *His hands.* He gazed down at them, glowing yellow-red in the firelight. The nails were black and chipped. Warts and endless calluses on each finger, and the palms. But they were good hands; the fingers were long and tapered. He respected them, although in some ways he didn't understand them.

Cole was deep in thought, meditating over his situation. He had been in the mountains two nights and a day. The first night had been the worst. Stumbling and falling, making his way uncertainly up the steep slopes, through the tangled brush and undergrowth...

But when the sun came up he was safe, deep in the mountains, between two great peaks. And by the time the sun had set again he had fixed himself up a shelter and a means of making a fire. Now he had a neat little box trap, operated by a plaited grass rope and pit, a notched stake. One rabbit already hung by his hind legs and the trap was waiting for another.

The sky turned from violet gray to a deep cold gray, a metallic color. The mountains were silent and empty. Far off some place a bird sang, its voice echoing across the vast slopes and ravines. Other birds began to sing. Off to his right something crashed through the brush, an animal pushing its way along.

Day was coming. His second day. Cole got to his feet and began to unfasten the rabbit. Time to eat. And then? After that he had no plans. He knew instinctively that he could keep himself alive indefinitely with the tools he had retained, and the genius of his hands. He could kill game and skin it. Eventually he could build himself a permanent shelter, even make clothes but of hides. In winter...

But he was not thinking that far ahead. Cole stood by the fire, staring up at the sky, his hands on his hips. He squinted, suddenly tense. Something was moving. Something in the sky, drifting slowly through the grayness. A black dot.

He stamped out the fire quickly. What was it? He strained, trying to see. A bird?

A second dot joined the first. Two dots. Then three. Four. Five. A fleet of them, moving rapidly across the early morning sky. Toward the mountains.

Toward him.

Cole hurried away from the fire. He snatched up the rabbit and carried it along with him, into the tangled shelter he had built. He was invisible, inside the shelter. No one could find him. But if they had seen the fire…

He crouched in the shelter, watching the dots grow larger. They were planes, all right. Black wingless planes, coming closer each moment. Now he could hear them, a faint dull buzz, increasing until the ground shook under him.

The first plane dived. It dropped like a stone, swelling into a great black shape. Cole gasped, sinking down. The plane roared in an arc, swooping low over the ground. Suddenly bundles tumbled out, white bundles falling and scattering like seeds.

The bundles drifted rapidly to the ground. They landed. They were men. Men in uniform.

Now the second plane was diving. It roared overhead, releasing its load. More bundles tumbled out, filling the sky. The third plane dived, then the fourth. The air was thick with drifting bundles of white, a blanket of descending weed spores, settling to earth.

On the ground the soldiers were forming into groups. Their shouts carried to Cole, crouched in his shelter. Fear leaped through him. They were landing on all sides of him. He was cut off. The last two planes had dropped men behind him.

He got to his feet, pushing out of the shelter. Some of the soldiers had found the fire, the ashes and coals. One dropped down, feeling the coals with his hand. He waved to the others. They were circling all around, shouting and gesturing. One of them began to set up some kind of gun. Others were unrolling coils of tubing, locking a collection of strange pipes and machinery in place.

Cole ran. He rolled down a slope, sliding and falling. At the bottom he leaped to his feet and plunged into the brush. Vines and leaves tore at his face, slashing and cutting him. He fell again, tangled in a mass of twisted shrubbery. He fought desperately, trying to free himself. If he could reach the knife in his pocket...

Voices. Footsteps. Men were behind him, running down the slope. Cole struggled frantically, gasping and twisting, trying to pull loose. He strained, breaking the vines, clawing at them with his hands.

A soldier dropped to his knee, leveling his gun. More soldiers arrived, bringing up their rifles and aiming.

Cole cried out. He closed his eyes, his body suddenly limp. He waited, his teeth locked together, sweat dripping down his neck, into his shirt, sagging against the mesh of vines and branches coiled around him.

Silence.

Cole opened his eyes slowly. The soldiers had regrouped. A huge man was striding down the slope toward them, barking orders as he came.

Two soldiers stepped into the brush. One of them grabbed Cole by the shoulder.

"Don't let go of him." The huge man came over, his black beard jutting out. "Hold on."

Cole gasped for breath. He was caught. There was nothing he could do. More soldiers were pouring down into the gulley, surrounding him on all sides. They studied him curiously, murmuring together. Cole shook his head wearily and said nothing.

The huge man with the beard stood directly in front of him, his hands on his hips, looking him up and down. "Don't try to get away," the man said. "You can't get away. Do you understand?"

Cole nodded.

"All right. Good." The man waved. Soldiers clamped metal bands around Cole's arms and wrists. The metal dug into his flesh, making him gasp with pain. More clamps locked around his legs. "Those stay there until we're out of here. A long way out."

"Where—where are you taking me?"

Peter Sherikov studied the variable man for a moment before he answered. "Where? I'm taking you to my labs. Under the Urals." He glanced suddenly up at the sky. "We better hurry. The Security police will be starting their demolition attack in a few hours. We want to be a long way from here when that begins."

Sherikov settled down in his comfortable reinforced chair with a sigh. "It's good to be back." He signaled to one of his guards. "All right. You can unfasten him."

The metal clamps were removed from Cole's arms and legs. He sagged, sinking down in a heap. Sherikov watched him silently.

Cole sat on the floor, rubbing his wrists and legs, saying nothing.

"What do you want?" Sherikov demanded. "Food? Are you hungry?"

"No."

"Medicine? Are you sick? Injured?"

"No."

Sherikov wrinkled his nose. "A bath wouldn't hurt you any. We'll arrange that later." He lit a cigar, blowing a cloud of gray smoke around him. At the door of the room two lab guards stood with guns ready. No one else was in the room beside Sherikov and Cole.

Thomas Cole sat huddled in a heap on the floor, his head sunk down against his chest. He did not stir. His bent body seemed more elongated and stooped than ever, his hair tousled and unkempt, his chin and jowls a rough stubbled gray. His clothes were dirty and torn from crawling through the brush. His skin was cut and scratched; open sores dotted his neck and cheeks and forehead. He said nothing. His chest rose and fell. His faded blue eyes were almost closed. He looked quite old, a withered, dried-up old man.

Sherikov waved one of the guards over. "Have a doctor brought up here. I want this man checked over. He may need intravenous injections. He may not have had anything to eat for awhile."

The guard departed.

"I don't want anything to happen to you," Sherikov said. "Before we go on I'll have you checked over. And deloused at the same time."

Cole said nothing.

Sherikov laughed. "Buck up! You have no reason to feel bad." He leaned toward Cole, jabbing an immense finger at him. "Another two hours and you'd have been dead, out there in the mountains. You know that?"

Cole nodded.

"You don't believe me. Look." Sherikov leaned over and snapped on the vidscreen mounted in the wall. "Watch, this. The operation should still be going on."

The screen lit up. A scene gained form.

"This is a confidential Security channel. I had it tapped several years ago—for my own protection. What we're seeing now is being piped in to Eric Reinhart." Sherikov grinned. "Reinhart arranged what you're seeing on the screen. Pay close attention. You were there, two hours ago."

Cole turned toward the screen. At first he could not make out what was happening. The screen showed a vast foaming cloud, a vortex of motion. From the speaker came a low rumble, a deep-throated roar. After a time the screen shifted, showing a slightly different view. Suddenly Cole stiffened.

He was seeing the destruction of a whole mountain range.

The picture was coming from a ship, flying above what had once been the Albertine Mountain Range. Now there was nothing but swirling clouds of gray and columns of particles and debris, a surging tide of restless material gradually sweeping off and dissipating in all directions.

The Albertine Mountains had been disintegrated. Nothing remained but these vast clouds of debris. Below, on the ground, a ragged plain stretched out, swept by fire and ruin. Gaping wounds yawned, immense holes without bottom, craters side by side as far as the eye could see. Craters and debris. Like the blasted, pitted surface of the moon. Two hours ago it had been rolling peaks and gullies, brush and green bushes and trees.

Cole turned away.

"You see?" Sherikov snapped the screen off. "You were down there, not so long ago. All that noise and smoke—all for you. All for you, Mr. Variable Man from the past. Reinhart arranged that, to finish you off. I want you to understand that. It's very important that you realize that."

Cole said nothing.

Sherikov reached into a drawer of the table before him. He carefully brought out a small square box and held it out to Cole. "You wired this, didn't you?"

Cole took the box in his hands and held it. For a time his tired mind failed to focus. What did he have? He concentrated on it. The box was the children's toy. The inter-system vidsender, they had called it.

"Yes. I fixed this." He passed it back to Sherikov. "I repaired that. It was broken."

Sherikov gazed down at him intently, his large eyes bright. He nodded, his black beard and cigar rising and falling. "Good. That's all I wanted to know." He got suddenly to his feet, pushing his chair back. "I see the doctor's here. He'll fix you up. Everything you need. Later on I'll talk to you again."

Unprotesting, Cole got to his feet, allowing the doctor to take hold of his arm and help him up.

After Cole had been released by the medical department, Sherikov joined him in his private dining room, a floor above the actual laboratory.

The Pole gulped down a hasty meal, talking as he ate. Cole sat silently across from him, not eating or speaking. His old clothing had been taken away and new clothing given him. He was shaved and rubbed down. His sores and cuts were healed, his body and hair washed. He looked much healthier and younger, now. But he was still stooped and tired, his blue eyes worn and faded. He listened to Sherikov's account of the world of 2136 AD without comment.

"You can see," Sherikov said finally, waving a chicken leg, "that your appearance here has been very upsetting to our program. Now that you know more about us you can see why Commissioner Reinhart was so interested in destroying you."

Cole nodded.

"Reinhart, you realize, believes that the failure of the SRB machines is the chief danger to the war effort. But that is nothing!" Sherikov pushed his plate away noisily, draining his coffee mug. "After all, wars *can* be fought without statistical forecasts. The SRB machines only describe. They're nothing more than mechanical onlookers. In themselves, they don't affect the course of the war. *We* make the war. They only analyze."

Cole nodded.

"More coffee?" Sherikov asked. He pushed the plastic container toward Cole. "Have some."

Cole accepted another cupful. "Thank you."

"You can see that our real problem is another thing entirely. The machines only do figuring for us in a few minutes that eventually we could do for our own selves. They're our servants, tools. Not some sort of gods in a temple which we go and pray to. Not oracles who can see into the future for us. They don't see into the future. They only make statistical predictions— not prophecies. There's a big difference there, but Reinhart doesn't understand it. Reinhart and his kind have made such things as the SRB machines into gods. But I have no gods. At least, not any I can see."

Cole nodded, sipping his coffee.

"I'm telling you all these things because you must understand what we're up against. Terra is hemmed in on all sides by the ancient Centauran Empire. It's been out there for centuries, thousands of years. No one knows how long. It's old—crumbling and rotting. Corrupt and venal. But it holds most of the galaxy around us, and we can't break out of the Sol system. I told you about Icarus, and Hedge's work in faster-than-light flight. We must win the war against Centaurus. We've waited and worked a long time for this, the moment when we can break out and get room among the stars for ourselves. Icarus is the deciding weapon. The data on Icarus tipped the SRB odds in our favor—for the first time in history. Success in the war against Centaurus will depend on Icarus, not on the SRB machines. You see?"

Cole nodded.

"However, there is a problem. The data on Icarus which I turned over to the machines specified that Icarus would be completed in ten days. More than half that time has already passed. Yet, we are no closer to wiring up the control turret than we were then. The turret baffles us." Sherikov grinned ironically. "Even *I* have tried my hand at the wiring, but with no success. It's intricate—and small. Too many technical bugs not worked out. We are building only one, you understand. If we had many experimental models worked out before—"

"But this is the experimental model," Cole said.

"And built from the designs of a man dead four years—who isn't here to correct us. We've made Icarus with our own hands, down here in the labs. And he's giving us plenty of trouble." All at once Sherikov got to his feet. "Let's go down to the lab and look at him."

They descended to the floor below, Sherikov leading the way. Cole stopped short at the lab door.

"Quite a sight," Sherikov agreed. "We keep him down here at the bottom for safety's sake. He's well protected. Come on in. We have work to do."

In the center of the lab Icarus rose up, the gray squat cylinder that someday would flash through space at a speed of thousands of times that of light, toward the heart of Proxima Centaurus, over four light years away. Around the cylinder groups of men in uniform were laboring feverishly to finish the remaining work.

"Over here. The turret." Sherikov led Cole over to one side of the room. "It's guarded. Centauran spies are swarming everywhere on Terra. They see into everything. But so do we. That's how we get information for the SRB machines. Spies in both systems."

The translucent globe that was the control turret reposed in the center of a metal stand, an armed guard standing at each side. They lowered their guns as Sherikov approached.

"We don't want anything to happen to this," Sherikov said. "Everything depends on it." He put out his hand for the globe. Half way to it his hand stopped, striking against an invisible presence in the air.

Sherikov laughed. "The wall. Shut it off. It's still on."

One of the guards pressed a stud at his wrist. Around the globe the air shimmered and faded.

"Now." Sherikov's hand closed over the globe. He lifted it carefully from its mount and brought it out for Cole to see. "This is the control turret for our enormous friend here. This is what will slow him down when he's inside Centaurus. He slows down and re-enters this universe. Right in the heart of the star. Then—no more Centaurus." Sherikov beamed. "And no more Armun."

But Cole was not listening. He had taken the globe from Sherikov and was turning it over and over, running his hands over it, his face close to its surface. He peered down into its interior, his face rapt and intent.

"You can't see the wiring. Not without lenses." Sherikov signaled for a pair of micro-lenses to be brought. He fitted them on Cole's nose, hooking them behind his ears. "Now try it. You can control the magnification. It's set for 1000X right now. You can increase or decrease it."

Cole gasped, swaying back and forth. Sherikov caught hold of him. Cole gazed down into the globe, moving his head slightly, focusing the glasses.

"It takes practice. But you can do a lot with them. Permits you to do microscopic wiring. There are tools to go along, you understand." Sherikov paused, licking his lip. "We can't get it done correctly. Only a few men can wire circuits using the micro-lenses and the little tools. We've tried robots, but there are too many decisions to be made. Robots can't make decisions. They just react."

Cole said nothing. He continued to gaze into the interior of the globe, his lips tight, his body taut and rigid. It made Sherikov feel strangely uneasy.

"You look like one of those old fortune tellers," Sherikov said jokingly, but a cold shiver crawled up his spine. "Better hand it back to me." He held out his hand.

Slowly, Cole returned the globe. After a time he removed the micro-lenses, still deep in thought.

"Well?" Sherikov demanded. "You know what I want. I want you to wire this damn thing up."

Sherikov came close to Cole, his big face hard. "You can do it, I think. I could tell by the way you held it—and the job you did on the children's toy, of course. You could wire it up right, and in five days. Nobody else can. And if it's not wired up Centaurus will keep on running the galaxy and Terra will have to sweat it out here in the Sol system. One tiny mediocre sun, one dust mote out of a whole galaxy."

Cole did not answer.

Sherikov became impatient. "Well? What do you say?"

"What happens if I don't wire this control for you? I mean, what happens to *me?*"

"Then I turn you over to Reinhart. Reinhart will kill you instantly. He thinks you're dead, killed when the Albertine Range was annihilated. If he had any idea I had saved you—"

"I see."

"I brought you down here for one thing. If you wire it up I'll have you sent back to your own time continuum. If you don't—"

Cole considered, his face dark and brooding.

"What do you have to lose? You'd already be dead, if we hadn't pulled you out of those hills."

"Can you really return me to my own time?"

"Of course!"

"Reinhart won't interfere?"

Sherikov laughed. "What can he do? How can he stop me? I have my own men. You saw them. They landed all around you. You'll be returned."

"Yes. I saw your men."

"Then you agree?"

"I agree," Thomas Cole said. "I'll wire it for you. I'll complete the control turret—within the next five days."

CHAPTER FOUR

Three days later Joseph Dixon slid a closed-circuit message plate across the desk to his boss.

"Here. You might be interested in this."

Reinhart picked the plate up slowly. "What is it? You came all the way here to show me this?"

"That's right."

"Why didn't you vidscreen it?"

Dixon smiled grimly. "You'll understand when you decode it. It's from Proxima Centaurus."

"Centaurus!"

"Our counter-intelligence service. They sent it direct to me. Here, I'll decode it for you. Save you the trouble."

Dixon came around behind Reinhart's desk. He leaned over the Commissioner's shoulder, taking hold of the plate and breaking the seal with his thumb nail.

"Hang on," Dixon said. "This is going to hit you hard. According to our agents on Armun, the Centauran High Council has called an emergency session to deal with the problem of Terra's impending attack. Centauran relay couriers have reported to the High Council that the Terran bomb Icarus is virtually complete. Work on the bomb has been rushed through final stages in the underground laboratories under the Ural Range, directed by the Terran physicist Peter Sherikov."

"So I understand from Sherikov himself. Are you surprised the Centaurans know about the bomb? They have spies swarming over Terra. That's no news."

"There's more." Dixon traced the message plate grimly, with an unsteady finger. "The Centauran relay couriers reported that Peter Sherikov brought an expert mechanic out of a previous time continuum to complete the wiring of the turret!"

Reinhart staggered, holding on tight to the desk. He closed his eyes, gasping.

"The variable man is still alive," Dixon murmured. "I don't know how. Or why. There's nothing left of the Albertines. And how the hell did the man get half way around the world?"

Reinhart opened his eyes slowly, his face twisting. "Sherikov! He must have removed him before the attack. I told Sherikov the attack was forthcoming. I gave him the exact hour. He had to get help—from the variable man. He couldn't meet his promise otherwise."

Reinhart leaped up and began to pace back and forth. "I've already informed the SRB machines that the variable man has been destroyed. The machines now show the original 7-6 ratio in our favor. But the ratio is based on false information."

"Then you'll have to withdraw the false data and restore the original situation."

"No." Reinhart shook his head. "I can't do that. The machines must be kept functioning. We can't allow them to jam again. It's too dangerous. If Duffe should become aware that—"

"What are you going to do, then?" Dixon picked up the message plate. "You can't leave the machines with false data. That's treason."

"The data can't be withdrawn! Not unless equivalent data exists to take its place." Reinhart paced angrily back and forth. "Damn it, I was *certain* the man was dead. This is an incredible situation. He must be eliminated—at any cost."

Suddenly Reinhart stopped pacing. "The turret. It's probably finished by this time. Correct?"

Dixon nodded slowly in agreement. "With the variable man helping, Sherikov has undoubtedly completed work well ahead of schedule."

Reinhart's gray eyes flickered. "Then he's no longer of any use—even to Sherikov. We could take a chance…. Even if there were active opposition…."

"What's this?" Dixon demanded. "What are you thinking about?"

"How many units are ready for immediate action? How large a force can we raise without notice?"

"Because of the war we're mobilized on a twenty-four hour basis. There are seventy air units and about two hundred surface units. The balance of the Security forces have been transferred to the line, under military control."

"Men?"

"We have about five thousand men ready to go, still on Terra. Most of them in the process of being transferred to military transports. I can hold it up at any time."

"Missiles?"

"Fortunately, the launching tubes have not yet been disassembled. They're still here on Terra. In another few days they'll be moving out for the Colonial fracas."

"Then they're available for immediate use?"

"Yes."

"Good." Reinhart locked his hands, knotting his fingers harshly together in sudden decision. "That will do exactly. Unless I am completely wrong, Sherikov has only a half-dozen air units and no surface cars. And only about two hundred men. Some defense shields, of course—"

"What are you planning?"

Reinhart's face was gray and hard, like stone. "Send out orders for all available Security units to be unified under your immediate command. Have them ready to move by four o'clock this afternoon. We're going to pay a visit," Reinhart stated grimly. "A surprise visit. On Peter Sherikov."

"Stop here," Reinhart ordered.

The surface car slowed to a halt. Reinhart peered cautiously out, studying the horizon ahead.

On all sides a desert of scrub grass and sand stretched out. Nothing moved or stirred. To the right the grass and sand rose up to form immense peaks, a range of mountains without end, disappearing finally into the distance. The Urals.

"Over there," Reinhart said to Dixon, pointing. "See?"

"No."

"Look hard. It's difficult to spot unless you know what to look for. Vertical pipes. Some kind of vent. Or periscopes."

Dixon saw them finally. "I would have driven past without noticing."

"It's well concealed. The main labs are a mile down. Under the range itself. It's virtually impregnable. Sherikov had it built years ago, to withstand any attack. From the air, by surface cars, bombs, missiles—"

"He must feel safe down there."

"No doubt." Reinhart gazed up at the sky. A few faint black dots could be seen, moving lazily about, in broad circles. "Those aren't ours, are they? I gave orders—"

"No. They're not ours. All our units are out of sight. Those belong to Sherikov. His patrol."

Reinhart relaxed. "Good." He reached over and flicked on the vidscreen over the board of the car. "This screen is shielded? It can't be traced?"

"There's no way they can spot it back to us. It's non-directional."

The screen glowed into life. Reinhart punched the combination keys and sat back to wait.

After a time an image formed on the screen. A heavy face, bushy black beard and large eyes.

Peter Sherikov gazed at Reinhart with surprised curiosity. "Commissioner! Where are you calling from? What—"

"How's the work progressing?" Reinhart broke in coldly. "Is Icarus almost complete?"

Sherikov beamed with expansive pride. "He's done, Commissioner. Two days ahead of time. Icarus is ready to be launched into space. I tried to call your office, but they told me—"

"I'm not at my office." Reinhart leaned toward the screen. "Open your entrance tunnel at the surface. You're about to receive visitors."

Sherikov blinked. "Visitors?"

"I'm coming down to see you. About Icarus. Have the tunnel opened for me at once."

"Exactly where are you, Commissioner?"

"On the surface."

Sherikov's eyes flickered. "Oh? But—"

"Open up!" Reinhart snapped. He glanced at his wristwatch. "I'll be at the entrance in five minutes. I expect to find it ready for me."

"Of course." Sherikov nodded in bewilderment. "I'm always glad to see you, Commissioner. But I—"

"Five minutes, then." Reinhart cut the circuit. The screen died. He turned quickly to Dixon. "You stay up here, as we arranged. I'll go down with one company of police. You understand the necessity of exact timing on this?"

"We won't slip up. Everything's ready. All units are in their places."

"Good." Reinhart pushed the door open for him. "You join your directional staff. I'll proceed toward the tunnel entrance."

"Good luck." Dixon leaped out of the car, onto the sandy ground. A gust of dry air swirled into the car around Reinhart. "I'll see you later."

Reinhart slammed the door. He turned to the group of police crouched in the rear of the car, their guns held tightly. "Here we go," Reinhart murmured. "Hold on."

The car raced across the sandy ground, toward the tunnel entrance to Sherikov's underground fortress.

Sherikov met Reinhart at the bottom end of the tunnel, where the tunnel opened up onto the main floor of the lab.

The big Pole approached, his hand out, beaming with pride and satisfaction. "It's a pleasure to see you, Commissioner. This is an historic moment."

Reinhart got out of the car, with his group of armed Security police. "Calls for a celebration, doesn't it?" he said.

"That's a good idea! We're two days ahead, Commissioner. The SRB machines will be interested. The odds should change abruptly at the news."

"Let's go down to the lab. I want to see the control turret myself."

A shadow crossed Sherikov's face. "I'd rather not bother the workmen right now, Commissioner. They've been under a great load, trying to complete the turret in time. I believe they're putting a few last finishes on it at this moment."

"We can view them by vidscreen. I'm curious to see them at work. It must be difficult to wire such minute relays."

Sherikov shook his head. "Sorry, Commissioner. No vidscreen on them. I won't allow it. This is too important. Our whole future depends on it."

Reinhart snapped a signal to his company of police. "Put this man under arrest."

Sherikov blanched. His mouth fell open. The police moved quickly around him, their gun tubes up, jabbing into him. He was searched rapidly, efficiently. His gun belt and concealed energy screen were yanked off.

"What's going on?" Sherikov demanded, some color returning to his face. "What are you doing?"

"You're under arrest for the duration of the war. You're relieved of all authority. From now on one of my men will operate Designs. When the war is over you'll be tried before the Council and President Duffe."

Sherikov shook his head, dazed. "I don't understand. What's this all about? Explain it to me, Commissioner. What's happened?"

Reinhart signaled to his police. "Get ready. We're going into the lab. We may have to shoot our way in. The variable man should be in the area of the bomb, working on the control turret."

Instantly Sherikov's face hardened. His black eyes glittered, alert and hostile.

Reinhart laughed harshly. "We received a counter-intelligence report from Centaurus. I'm surprised at you, Sherikov. You know the Centaurans are everywhere with their relay couriers. You should have known—"

Sherikov moved. Fast. All at once he broke away from the police, throwing his massive body against them. They fell, scattering. Sherikov ran—directly at the wall. The police fired wildly. Reinhart fumbled frantically for his gun tube, pulling it up.

Sherikov reached the wall, running head down, energy beams flashing around him. He struck against the wall—and vanished.

"Down!" Reinhart shouted. He dropped to his hands and knees. All around him his police dived for the floor. Reinhart cursed wildly, dragging himself quickly toward the door. They had to get out, and right away. Sherikov had escaped. A false wall, an energy barrier set to respond to his pressure. He had dashed through it to safety. He...

From all sides an inferno burst, a flaming roar of death surging over them, around them, on every side. The room was alive with blazing masses of destruction, bouncing from wall to wall. They were caught between four banks of power, all of them open to full discharge. A trap—a death trap.

Reinhart reached the hall gasping for breath. He leaped to his feet. A few Security police followed him. Behind them, in the flaming room, the rest of the company screamed and struggled, blasted out of existence by the leaping bursts of power.

Reinhart assembled his remaining men. Already, Sherikov's guards were forming. At one end of the corridor a snub-barreled robot gun was maneuvering into position. A siren wailed. Guards were running on all sides, hurrying to battle stations.

The robot gun opened fire. Part of the corridor exploded, bursting into fragments. Clouds of choking debris and particles swept around them. Reinhart and his police retreated, moving back along the corridor.

They reached a junction. A second robot gun was rumbling toward them, hurrying to get within range. Reinhart fired carefully, aiming at its delicate control. Abruptly the gun spun convulsively. It lashed against the wall, smashing itself into the unyielding metal. Then it collapsed in a heap, gears still whining and spinning.

"Come on." Reinhart moved away, crouching and running. He glanced at his watch. *Almost time.* A few more minutes. A group of lab guards appeared ahead of them. Reinhart fired. Behind him his police fired past him, violet shafts of energy catching the group of guards as they entered the corridor. The guards spilled apart, falling and twisting. Part of them settled into dust, drifting down the corridor. Reinhart made his way toward the lab, crouching and leaping, pushing past heaps of debris and remains, followed by his men. "Come on! Don't stop!"

Suddenly from around them the booming, enlarged voice of Sherikov thundered, magnified by rows of wall speakers along the corridor. Reinhart halted, glancing around.

"Reinhart! You haven't got a chance. You'll never get back to the surface. Throw down your guns and give up. You're surrounded on all sides. You're a mile, under the surface."

Reinhart threw himself into motion, pushing into billowing clouds of particles drifting along the corridor. "Are you sure, Sherikov?" he grunted.

Sherikov laughed, his harsh, metallic peals rolling in waves against Reinhart's eardrums. "I don't want to have to kill you, Commissioner. You're vital to the war: I'm sorry you found out about the variable man. I admit we overlooked the Centauran espionage as a factor in this. But now that you know about him—"

Suddenly Sherikov's voice broke off. A deep rumble had shaken the floor, a lapping vibration that shuddered through the corridor.

Reinhart sagged with relief. He peered through the clouds of debris, making out the figures on his watch. Right on time. Not a second late.

The first of the hydrogen missiles, launched from the Council buildings on the other side of the world, were beginning to arrive. The attack had begun.

At exactly six o'clock Joseph Dixon, standing on the surface four miles from the entrance tunnel, gave the sign to the waiting units.

The first job was to break down Sherikov's defense screens. The missiles had to penetrate without interference. At Dixon's signal a fleet of thirty Security ships dived from a height of ten miles, swooping above the mountains, directly over the underground laboratories. Within five minutes the defense screens had been smashed, and all the tower projectors leveled flat. Now the mountains were virtually unprotected.

"So far so good," Dixon murmured, as he watched from his secure position. The fleet of Security ships roared back, their work done. Across the face of the desert the police surface cars were crawling rapidly toward the entrance tunnel, snaking from side to side.

Meanwhile, Sherikov's counter-attack had begun to go into operation.

Guns mounted among the hills opened fire. Vast columns of flame burst up in the path of the advancing cars. The cars hesitated and retreated, as the plain was churned up by a howling vortex, a thundering chaos of explosions. Here and there a car vanished in a cloud of particles. A group of cars moving away suddenly scattered, caught up by a giant wind that lashed across them and swept them up into the air.

Dixon gave orders to have the cannon silenced. The police air arm again swept overhead, a sullen roar of jets that shook the ground below. The police ships divided expertly and hurtled down on the cannon protecting the hills.

The cannon forgot the surface cars and lifted their snouts to meet the attack. Again and again the airships came, rocking the mountains with titanic blasts.

The guns became silent. Their echoing boom diminished, died away reluctantly, as bombs took critical toll of them.

Dixon watched with satisfaction as the bombing came to an end. The airships rose in a thick swarm, black gnats shooting up in triumph from a dead carcass. They hurried back as emergency anti-aircraft robot guns swung into position and saturated the sky with blazing puffs of energy.

Dixon checked his wristwatch. The missiles were already on the way from North America. Only a few minutes remained.

The surface cars, freed by the successful bombing, began to regroup for a new frontal attack. Again they crawled forward, across the burning plain, bearing down cautiously on the battered wall of mountains, heading toward the twisted wrecks that had been the ring of defense guns. Toward the entrance tunnel.

An occasional cannon fired feebly at them. The cars came grimly on. Now, in the hollows of the hills, Sherikov's troops were hurrying to the surface to meet the attack. The first car reached the shadow of the mountains....

A deafening hail of fire burst loose. Small robot guns appeared everywhere, needle barrels emerging from behind hidden screens, trees and shrubs, rocks, stones. The police cars were caught in a withering cross-fire, trapped at the base of the hills.

Down the slopes Sherikov's guards raced, toward the stalled cars. Clouds of heat rose up and boiled across the plain as the cars fired up at the running men. A robot gun dropped like a slug onto the plain and screamed toward the cars, firing as it came.

Dixon twisted nervously. Only a few minutes. Any time, now. He shaded his eyes and peered up at the sky. No sign of them yet. He wondered about

Reinhart. No signal had come up from below. Clearly, Reinhart had run into trouble. No doubt there was desperate fighting going on in the maze of underground tunnels, the intricate web of passages that honeycombed the earth below the mountains.

In the air, Sherikov's few defense ships were taking on the police raiders. Outnumbered, the defense ships darted rapidly, wildly, putting up a futile fight.

Sherikov's guards streamed out onto the plain. Crouching and running, they advanced toward the stalled cars. The police airships screeched down at them, guns thundering.

Dixon held his breath. When the missiles arrived…

The first missile struck. A section of the mountain vanished, turned to smoke and foaming gasses. The wave of heat slapped Dixon across the face, spinning him around. Quickly he re-entered his ship and took off, shooting rapidly away from the scene. He glanced back. A second and third missile had arrived. Great gaping pits yawned among the mountains, vast sections missing like broken teeth. Now the missiles could penetrate to the underground laboratories below.

On the ground, the surface cars halted beyond the danger area, waiting for the missile attack to finish. When the eighth missile had struck, the cars again moved forward. No more missiles fell.

Dixon swung his ship around, heading back toward the scene. The laboratory was exposed. The top sections of it had been ripped open. The laboratory lay like a tin can, torn apart by mighty explosions, its first floors visible from the air. Men and cars were pouring down into it, fighting with the guards swarming to the surface.

Dixon watched intently. Sherikov's men were bringing up heavy guns, big robot artillery. But the police ships were diving again. Sherikov's defensive patrols had been cleaned from the sky. The police ships whined down, arcing over the exposed laboratory. Small bombs fell, whistling down, pinpointing the artillery rising to the surface on the remaining lift stages.

Abruptly Dixon's vidscreen clicked. Dixon turned toward it.

Reinhart's features formed. "Call off the attack." His uniform was torn. A deep bloody gash crossed his cheek. He grinned sourly at Dixon, pushing his tangled hair back out of his face. "Quite a fight."

"Sherikov—"

"He's called off his guards. We've agreed to a truce. It's all over. No more needed." Reinhart gasped for breath, wiping grime and sweat from his neck. "Land your ship and come down here at once."

"The variable man?"

"That comes next," Reinhart said grimly. He adjusted his gun tube. "I want you down here, for that part. I want you to be in on the kill."

Reinhart turned away from the vidscreen. In the corner of the room Sherikov stood silently, saying nothing. "Well?" Reinhart barked. "Where is he? Where will I find him?"

Sherikov licked his lips nervously, glancing up at Reinhart. "Commissioner, are you sure—"

"The attack has been called off. Your labs are safe. So is your life. Now it's your turn to come through." Reinhart gripped his gun, moving toward Sherikov. *"Where is he?"*

For a moment Sherikov hesitated. Then slowly his huge body sagged, defeated. He shook his head wearily. "All right. I'll show you where he is." His voice was hardly audible, a dry whisper. "Down this way. Come on."

Reinhart followed Sherikov out of the room, into the corridor. Police and guards were working rapidly, clearing the debris and ruins away, putting out the hydrogen fires that burned everywhere. "No tricks, Sherikov."

"No tricks." Sherikov nodded resignedly. "Thomas Cole is by himself. In a wing lab off the main rooms."

"Cole?"

"The variable man. That's his name." The Pole turned his massive head a little. "He has a name."

Reinhart waved his gun. "Hurry up. I don't want anything to go wrong. This is the part I came for."

"You must remember something, Commissioner."

"What is it?"

Sherikov stopped walking. "Commissioner, nothing must happen to the globe. The control turret. Everything depends on it, the war, our whole—"

"I know. Nothing will happen to the damn thing. Let's go."

"If it should get damaged—"

"I'm not after the globe. I'm interested only in—in Thomas Cole."

They came to the end of the corridor and stopped before a metal door. Sherikov nodded at the door. "In there."

Reinhart moved back. "Open the door."

"Open it yourself. I don't want to have anything to do with it."

Reinhart shrugged. He stepped up to the door. Holding his gun level he raised his hand, passing it in front of the eye circuit. Nothing happened.

Reinhart frowned. He pushed the door with his hand. The door slid open. Reinhart was looking into a small laboratory. He glimpsed a workbench, tools, heaps of equipment, measuring devices, and in the center of the bench the transparent globe, the control turret.

"Cole?" Reinhart advanced quickly into the room. He glanced around him, suddenly alarmed. "Where—"

The room was empty. Thomas Cole was gone.

When the first missile struck, Cole stopped work and sat listening.

Far off, a distant rumble rolled through the earth, shaking the floor under him. On the bench, tools and equipment danced up and down. A pair of pliers fell crashing to the floor. A box of screws tipped over, spilling its minute contents out.

Cole listened for a time. Presently he lifted the transparent globe from the bench. With carefully controlled hands he held the globe up, running his fingers gently over the surface, his faded blue eyes thoughtful. Then, after a time, he placed the globe back on the bench, in its mount.

The globe was finished. A faint glow of pride moved through the variable man. The globe was the finest job he had ever done.

The deep rumblings ceased. Cole became instantly alert. He jumped down from his stool, hurrying across the room to the door. For a moment he stood by the door listening intently. He could hear noise on the other side, shouts, guards rushing past, dragging heavy equipment, working frantically.

A rolling crash echoed down the corridor and lapped against his door. The concussion spun him around. Again a tide of energy shook the walls and floor and sent him down on his knees.

The lights flickered and winked out.

Cole fumbled in the dark until he found a flashlight. Power failure. He could hear crackling flames. Abruptly the lights came on again, an ugly yellow, then faded back out. Cole bent down and examined the door with his flashlight. A magnetic lock. Dependent on an externally induced electric flux. He grabbed a screwdriver and pried at the door. For a moment it held. Then it fell open.

Cole stepped warily out into the corridor. Everything was in shambles. Guards wandered everywhere, burned and half-blinded. Two lay groaning under a pile of wrecked equipment. Fused guns, reeking metal. The air was heavy with the smell of burning wiring and plastic. A thick cloud that choked him and made him bend double as he advanced.

"Halt," a guard gasped feebly, struggling to rise. Cole pushed past him and down the corridor. Two small robot guns, still functioning, glided past him hurriedly toward the drumming chaos of battle. He followed.

At a major intersection the fight was in full swing. Sherikov's guards fought Security police, crouched behind pillars and barricades, firing wildly, desperately. Again the whole structure shuddered as a great booming blast ignited some place above. Bombs? Shells?

Cole threw himself down as a violet beam cut past his ear and disintegrated the wall behind him. A Security policeman, wild-eyed, firing erratically. One of Sherikov's guards winged him and his gun skidded to the floor.

A robot cannon turned toward him as he made his way past the intersection. He began to run. The cannon rolled along behind him, aiming itself uncertainly. Cole hunched over as he shambled rapidly along, gasping for breath. In the flickering yellow light he saw a handful of Security police advancing, firing expertly, intent on a line of defense Sherikov's guards had hastily set up.

The robot cannon altered its course to take them on, and Cole escaped around a corner.

He was in the main lab, the big chamber where Icarus himself rose, the vast squat column.

Icarus! A solid wall of guards surrounded him, grim-faced, hugging guns and protection shields. But the Security police were leaving Icarus alone. Nobody wanted to damage him. Cole evaded a lone guard tracking him and reached the far side of the lab.

It took him only a few seconds to find the force field generator. There was no switch. For a moment that puzzled him—and then he remembered. The guard had controlled it from his wrist.

Too late to worry about that. With his screwdriver he unfastened the plate over the generator and ripped out the wiring in handfuls. The generator came loose and he dragged it away from the wall. The screen was off, thank God. He managed to carry the generator into a side corridor.

Crouched in a heap, Cole bent over the generator, deft fingers flying. He pulled the wiring to him and laid it out on the floor, tracing the circuits with feverish haste.

The adaptation was easier than he had expected. The screen flowed at right angles to the wiring, for a distance of six feet. Each lead was shielded on one side; the field radiated outward, leaving a hollow cone in the center. He ran the wiring through his belt, down his trouser legs, under his shirt, all the way to his wrists and ankles.

He was just snatching up the heavy generator when two Security police appeared. They raised their blasters and fired point-blank.

Cole clicked on the screen. A vibration leaped through him that snapped his jaw and danced up his body.   He staggered away, half-stupefied by the surging force that radiated out from him.   The violet rays struck the field and deflected harmlessly.

He was safe.

He hurried on down the corridor, past a ruined gun and sprawled bodies still clutching blasters.   Great drifting clouds of radioactive particles billowed around him.   He edged by one cloud nervously.   Guards lay everywhere, dying and dead, partly destroyed, eaten and corroded by the hot metallic salts in the air.   He had to get out—and fast.

At the end of the corridor a whole section of the fortress was in ruins.   Towering flames leaped on all sides.   One of the missiles had penetrated below ground level.

Cole found a lift that still functioned.   A load of wounded guards was being raised to the surface.   None of them paid any attention to him.   Flames surged around the lift, licking at the wounded.   Workmen were desperately trying to get the lift into action.   Cole leaped onto the lift.   A moment later it began to rise, leaving the shouts and the flames behind.

The lift emerged on the surface and Cole jumped off.   A guard spotted him and gave chase.   Crouching, Cole dodged into a tangled mass of twisted metal, still white-hot and smoking.   He ran for a distance, leaping from the side of a ruined defense-screen tower, onto the fused ground and down the side of a hill.   The ground was hot underfoot.   He hurried as fast as he could, gasping for breath. He came to a long slope and scrambled up the side.

The guard who had followed was gone, lost behind in the rolling clouds of ash that drifted from the ruins of Sherikov's underground fortress.

Cole reached the top of the hill. For a brief moment he halted to get his breath and figure where he was. It was almost evening. The sun was beginning to set. In the darkening sky a few dots still twisted and rolled, black specks that abruptly burst into flame and fused out again.

Cole stood up cautiously, peering around him. Ruins stretched out below, on all sides, the furnace from which he had escaped. A chaos of incandescent metal and debris, gutted and wrecked beyond repair. Miles of tangled rubbish and half-vaporized equipment.

He considered. Everyone was busy putting out the fires and pulling the wounded to safety. It would be awhile before he was missed. But as soon as they realized he was gone they'd be after him. Most of the laboratory had been destroyed. Nothing lay back that way.

Beyond the ruins lay the great Ural peaks, the endless mountains, stretching out as far as the eye could see.

Mountains and green forests. A wilderness. They'd never find him there.

Cole started along the side of the hill, walking slowly and carefully, his screen generator under his arm. Probably in the confusion he could find enough food and equipment to last him indefinitely. He could wait until early morning, then circle back toward the ruins and load up. With a few tools and his own innate skill he would get along fine. A screwdriver, hammer, nails, odds and ends...

A great hum sounded in his ears. It swelled to a deafening roar. Startled, Cole whirled around. A vast shape filled the sky behind him, growing each moment. Cole stood frozen, utterly transfixed. The shape thundered over him, above his head, as he stood stupidly, rooted to the spot.

Then, awkwardly, uncertainly, he began to run. He stumbled and fell and rolled a short distance down the side of the hill. Desperately, he struggled to hold onto the ground. His hands dug wildly, futilely, into the soft soil, trying to keep the generator under his arm at the same time.

A flash, and a blinding spark of light around him.

The spark picked him up and tossed him like a dry leaf. He grunted in agony as searing fire crackled about him, a blazing inferno that gnawed and ate hungrily through his screen. He spun dizzily and fell through the cloud of fire, down into a pit of darkness, a vast gulf between two hills. His wiring ripped off. The generator tore out of his grip and was lost behind. Abruptly, his force field ceased.

Cole lay in the darkness at the bottom of the hill. His whole body shrieked in agony as the unholy fire played over him. He was a blazing cinder, a half-consumed ash flaming in a universe of darkness. The pain made him twist and crawl like an insect, trying to burrow into the ground. He screamed and shrieked and struggled to escape, to get away from the hideous fire. To reach the curtain of darkness beyond, where it was cool and silent, where the flames couldn't crackle and eat at him.

He reached imploringly out, into the darkness, groping feebly toward it, trying to pull himself into it. Gradually, the glowing orb that was his own body faded. The impenetrable chaos of night descended. He allowed the tide to sweep over him, to extinguish the searing fire.

Dixon landed his ship expertly, bringing it to a halt in front of an overturned defense tower. He leaped out and hurried across the smoking ground.

From a lift Reinhart appeared, surrounded by his Security police. "He got away from us! He escaped!"

"He didn't escape," Dixon answered. "I got him myself."

Reinhart quivered violently. "What do you mean?"

"Come along with me. Over in this direction." He and Reinhart climbed the side of a demolished hill, both of them panting for breath. "I was landing. I saw a figure emerge from a lift and run toward the mountains, like some sort of animal. When he came out in the open I dived on him and released a phosphorus bomb."

"Then he's—*dead?*"

"I don't see how anyone could have lived through a phosphorus bomb." They reached the top of the hill. Dixon halted, then pointed excitedly down into the pit beyond the hill. "There!"

They descended cautiously. The ground was singed and burned clean. Clouds of smoke hung heavily in the air. Occasional fires still flickered here and there. Reinhart coughed and bent over to see. Dixon flashed on a pocket flare and set it beside the body.

The body was charred, half destroyed by the burning phosphorus. It lay motionless, one arm over its face, mouth open, legs sprawled grotesquely. Like some abandoned rag doll, tossed in an incinerator and consumed almost beyond recognition.

"He's alive!" Dixon muttered. He felt around curiously. "Must have had some kind of protection screen. Amazing that a man could—"

"It's him? It's really him?"

"Fits the description." Dixon tore away a handful of burned clothing. "This is the variable man. What's left of him, at least."

Reinhart sagged with relief. "Then we've finally got him. The data is accurate. He's no longer a factor."

Dixon got out his blaster and released the safety catch thoughtfully. "If you want, I can finish the job right now."

At that moment Sherikov appeared, accompanied by two armed Security police. He strode grimly down the hillside, black eyes snapping. "Did Cole—" He broke off. "Good God."

"Dixon got him with a phosphorus bomb," Reinhart said noncommittally. "He had reached the surface and was trying to get into the mountains."

Sherikov turned wearily away. "He was an amazing person. During the attack he managed to force the lock on his door and escape. The guards fired at him, but nothing happened. He had rigged up some kind of force field around him. Something he adapted."

"Anyhow, it's over with," Reinhart answered. "Did you have SRB plates made up on him?"

Sherikov reached slowly into his coat. He drew out a manila envelope. "Here's all the information I collected about him, while he was with me."

"Is it complete? Everything previous has been merely fragmentary."

"As near complete as I could make it. It includes photographs and diagrams of the interior of the globe. The turret wiring he did for me. I haven't had a chance even to look at them." Sherikov fingered the envelope. "What are you going to do with Cole?"

"Have him loaded up, taken back to the city—and officially put to sleep by the Euthanasia Ministry."

"Legal murder?" Sherikov's lips twisted. "Why don't you simply do it right here and get it over with?"

Reinhart grabbed the envelope and stuck it in his pocket. "I'll turn this right over to the machines." He motioned to Dixon. "Let's go. Now we can notify the fleet to prepare for the attack on Centaurus." He turned briefly back to Sherikov. "When can Icarus be launched?"

"In an hour or so, I suppose. They're locking the control turret in place. Assuming it functions correctly, that's all that's needed."

"Good. I'll notify Duffe to send out the signal to the war fleet." Reinhart nodded to the police to take Sherikov to the waiting Security ship. Sherikov moved off dully, his face gray and haggard. Cole's inert body was picked up and tossed onto a freight cart. The cart rumbled into the hold of the Security ship and the lock slid shut after it.

"It'll be interesting to see how the machines respond to the additional data," Dixon said.

"It should make quite an improvement in the odds," Reinhart agreed. He patted the envelope, bulging in his inside pocket. "We're two days ahead of time."

Margaret Duffe got up slowly from her desk. She pushed her chair automatically back. "Let me get all this straight. You mean the bomb is finished? Ready to go?"

Reinhart nodded impatiently. "That's what I said. The Technicians are checking the turret locks to make sure it's properly attached. The launching will take place in half an hour."

"Thirty minutes! Then—"

"Then the attack can begin at once. I assume the fleet is ready for action."

"Of course. It's been ready for several days. But I can't believe the bomb is ready so soon." Margaret Duffe moved numbly toward the door of her office. "This is a great day, Commissioner. An old era lies behind us. This time tomorrow Centaurus will be gone. And eventually the colonies will be ours."

"It's been a long climb," Reinhart murmured.

"One thing. Your charge against Sherikov. It seems incredible that a person of his caliber could ever—"

"We'll discuss that later," Reinhart interrupted coldly. He pulled the manila envelope from his coat. "I haven't had an opportunity to feed the additional data to the SRB machines. If you'll excuse me, I'll do that now."

For a moment Margaret Duffe stood at the door. The two of them faced each other silently, neither speaking, a faint smile on Reinhart's thin lips, hostility in the woman's blue eyes.

"Reinhart, sometimes I think perhaps you'll go too far. And sometimes I think you've *already* gone too far...."

"I'll inform you of any change in the odds showing." Reinhart strode past her, out of the office and down the hall. He headed toward the SRB room, an intense thalamic excitement rising up inside him.

A few moments later he entered the SRB room. He made his way to the machines. The odds 7-6 showed in the view windows. Reinhart smiled a little. 7-6. False odds, based on incorrect information. Now they could be removed.

Kaplan hurried over. Reinhart handed him the envelope, and moved over to the window, gazing down at the scene below. Men and cars scurried frantically everywhere. Officials coming and going like ants, hurrying in all directions.

The war was on. The signal had been sent out to the war fleet that had waited so long near Proxima Centaurus. A feeling of triumph raced through Reinhart. He had won. He had destroyed the man from the past and broken Peter Sherikov. The war had begun as planned. Terra was breaking out. Reinhart smiled thinly. He had been completely successful.

"Commissioner."

Reinhart turned slowly. "All right."

Kaplan was standing in front of the machines, gazing down at the reading. "Commissioner—"

Sudden alarm plucked at Reinhart. There was something in Kaplan's voice. He hurried quickly over. "What is it?"

Kaplan looked up at him, his face white, his eyes wide with terror. His mouth opened and closed, but no sound came.

"*What is it?*" Reinhart demanded, chilled. He bent toward the machines, studying the reading.

And sickened with horror.

100-1. *Against* Terra!

He could not tear his gaze away from the figures. He was numb, shocked with disbelief. 100-1. *What had happened?* What had gone wrong? The turret was finished, Icarus was ready, the fleet had been notified…

There was a sudden deep buzz from outside the building. Shouts drifted up from below. Reinhart turned his head slowly toward the window, his heart frozen with fear.

Across the evening sky a trail moved, rising each moment. A thin line of white. Something climbed, gaining speed each moment. On the ground, all eyes were turned toward it, awed faces peering up.

The object gained speed. Faster and faster. Then it vanished. Icarus was on his way. The attack had begun; it was too late to stop, now.

And on the machines the odds read a hundred to one—for failure.

At eight o'clock in the evening of May 15, 2136, Icarus was launched toward the star Centaurus. A day later, while all Terra waited, Icarus entered the star, traveling at thousands of times the speed of light.

Nothing happened. Icarus disappeared into the star. There was no explosion. The bomb failed to go off.

At the same time the Terran war fleet engaged the Centauran outer fleet, sweeping down in a concentrated attack. Twenty major ships were seized. A good part of the Centauran fleet was destroyed. Many of the captive systems began to revolt, in the hope of throwing off the Imperial bonds.

Two hours later the massed Centauran war fleet from Armun abruptly appeared and joined battle. The great struggle illuminated half the Centauran system. Ship after ship flashed briefly and then faded to ash. For a whole day the two fleets fought, strung out over millions of miles of space. Innumerable fighting men died—on both sides.

At last the remains of the battered Terran fleet turned and limped toward Armun—defeated. Little of the once impressive armada remained. A few blackened hulks, making their way uncertainly toward captivity.

Icarus had not functioned. Centaurus had not exploded. The attack was a failure.

The war was over.

"We've lost the war," Margaret Duffe said in a small voice, wondering and awed. "It's over. Finished."

The Council members sat in their places around the conference table, gray-haired elderly men, none of them speaking or moving. All gazed up mutely at the great stellar maps that covered two walls of the chamber.

"I have already empowered negotiators to arrange a truce," Margaret Duffe murmured. "Orders have been sent out to Vice-Commander Jessup to give up the battle. There's no hope. Fleet Commander Carleton destroyed himself and his flagship a few minutes ago. The Centauran High Council has agreed to end the fighting. Their whole Empire is rotten to the core. Ready to topple of its own weight."

Reinhart was slumped over at the table, his head in his hands. "I don't understand.... *Why?* Why didn't the bomb explode?" He mopped his forehead shakily. All his poise was gone. He was trembling and broken. "*What went wrong?*"

Gray-faced, Dixon mumbled an answer. "The variable man must have sabotaged the turret. The SRB machines knew.... They analyzed the data. *They knew!* But it was too late."

Reinhart's eyes were bleak with despair as he raised his head a little. "I knew he'd destroy us. We're finished. A century of work and planning." His body knotted in a spasm of furious agony. "All because of Sherikov!"

Margaret Duffe eyed Reinhart coldly. "Why because of Sherikov?"

"He kept Cole alive! I wanted him killed from the start." Suddenly Reinhart jumped from his chair. His hand clutched convulsively at his gun. "And he's *still* alive! Even if we've lost I'm going to have the pleasure of putting a blast beam through Cole's chest!"

"Sit down!" Margaret Duffe ordered.

Reinhart was half way to the door. "He's still at the Euthanasia Ministry, waiting for the official—"

"No, he's not," Margaret Duffe said.

Reinhart froze. He turned slowly, as if unable to believe his senses. "*What?*"

"Cole isn't at the Ministry. I ordered him transferred and your instructions cancelled."

"Where—where is he?"

There was unusual hardness in Margaret Duffe's voice as she answered. "With Peter Sherikov. In the Urals. I had Sherikov's full authority restored. I then had Cole transferred there, put in Sherikov's safe keeping. I want to make sure Cole recovers, so we can keep our promise to him—our promise to return him to his own time."

Reinhart's mouth opened and closed. All the color had drained from his face. His cheek muscles twitched spasmodically. At last he managed to speak. "You've gone insane! The traitor responsible for Earth's greatest defeat—"

"We have lost the war," Margaret Duffe stated quietly. "But this is not a day of defeat. It is a day of victory. The most incredible victory Terra has ever had."

Reinhart and Dixon were dumbfounded. "What—" Reinhart gasped. "What do you—" The whole room was in an uproar. All the Council members were on their feet. Reinhart's words were drowned out.

"Sherikov will explain when he gets here," Margaret Duffe's calm voice came. "He's the one who discovered it." She looked around the chamber at the incredulous Council members. "Everyone stay in his seat. You are all to remain here until Sherikov arrives. It's vital you hear what he has to say. His news transforms this whole situation."

Peter Sherikov accepted the briefcase of papers from his armed technician. "Thanks." He pushed his chair back and glanced thoughtfully around the Council chamber. "Is everybody ready to hear what I have to say?"

"We're ready," Margaret Duffe answered. The Council members sat alertly around the table. At the far end, Reinhart and Dixon watched uneasily as the big Pole removed papers from his briefcase and carefully examined them.

"To begin, I recall to you the original work behind the faster-than-light bomb. Jamison Hedge was the first human to propel an object at a speed greater than light. As you know, that object diminished in length and gained in mass as it moved toward light speed. When it reached that speed it vanished. It ceased to exist in our terms. Having no length it could not occupy space. It rose to a different order of existence.

"When Hedge tried to bring the object back, an explosion occurred. Hedge was killed, and all his equipment was destroyed. The force of the blast was beyond calculation. Hedge had placed his observation ship many millions of miles away. It was not far enough, however. Originally, he had hoped his drive might be used for space travel. But after his death the principle was abandoned.

"That is—until Icarus. I saw the possibilities of a bomb, an incredibly powerful bomb to destroy Centaurus and all the Empire's forces. The reappearance of Icarus would mean the annihilation of their System. As Hedge had shown, the object would re-enter space already occupied by matter, and the cataclysm would be beyond belief."

"But Icarus never came back," Reinhart cried. "Cole altered the wiring so the bomb kept on going. It's probably still going."

"Wrong," Sherikov boomed. "The bomb *did* reappear. But it didn't explode."

Reinhart reacted violently. "You mean—"

"The bomb came back, dropping below the faster-than-light speed as soon as it entered the star Proxima. But it did not explode. There was no cataclysm. It reappeared and was absorbed by the sun, turned into gas at once."

"Why didn't it explode?" Dixon demanded.

"Because Thomas Cole solved Hedge's problem. He found a way to bring the faster-than-light object back into this universe without collision. Without an explosion. The variable man found what Hedge was after...."

The whole Council was on its feet. A growing murmur filled the chamber, a rising pandemonium breaking out on all sides.

"I don't believe it!" Reinhart gasped. "It isn't possible. If Cole solved Hedge's problem that would mean—" He broke off, staggered.

"Faster than light drive can now be used for space travel," Sherikov continued, waving the noise down. "As Hedge intended. My men have studied the photographs of the control turret. They don't know *how* or *why*, yet. But we have complete records of the turret. We can duplicate the wiring, as soon as the laboratories have been repaired."

Comprehension was gradually beginning to settle over the room. "Then it'll be possible to build faster-than-light ships," Margaret Duffe murmured, dazed. "And if we can do that—"

"When I showed him the control turret, Cole understood its purpose. Not *my* purpose, but the original purpose Hedge had been working toward. Cole realized Icarus was actually an incomplete spaceship, not a bomb at all. He saw what Hedge had seen, an faster-than-light space drive. He set out to make Icarus work."

"We can go *beyond* Centaurus," Dixon muttered. His lips twisted. "Then the war was trivial. We can leave the Empire completely behind. We can go beyond the galaxy."

"The whole universe is open to us," Sherikov agreed. "Instead of taking over an antiquated Empire, we have the entire cosmos to map and explore, God's total creation."

Margaret Duffe got to her feet and moved slowly toward the great stellar maps that towered above them at the far end of the chamber. She stood for a long time, gazing up at the myriad suns, the legions of systems, awed by what she saw.

"Do you suppose he realized all this?" she asked suddenly. "What we can see, here on these maps?"

"Thomas Cole is a strange person," Sherikov said, half to himself. "Apparently he has a kind of intuition about machines, the way things are supposed to work. An intuition more in his hands than in his head. A kind of genius, such as a painter or a pianist has. Not a scientist. He has no verbal knowledge about things, no semantic references. He deals with the things themselves. Directly.

"I doubt very much if Thomas Cole understood what would come about. He looked into the globe, the control turret. He saw unfinished wiring and relays. He saw a job half done. An incomplete machine."

"Something to be fixed," Margaret Duffe put in.

"Something to be fixed. Like an artist, he saw his work ahead of him. He was interested in only one thing: turning out the best job he could, with the skill he possessed. For us, that skill has opened up a whole universe, endless galaxies and systems to explore. Worlds without end. Unlimited, *untouched* worlds."

Reinhart got unsteadily to his feet. "We better get to work. Start organizing construction teams. Exploration crews. We'll have to reconvert from war production to ship designing. Begin the manufacture of mining and scientific instruments for survey work."

"That's right," Margaret Duffe said. She looked reflectively up at him. "But you're not going to have anything to do with it."

Reinhart saw the expression on her face. His hand flew to his gun and he backed quickly toward the door. Dixon leaped up and joined him. "Get back!" Reinhart shouted.

Margaret Duffe signaled and a phalanx of Government troops closed in around the two men. Grim-faced, efficient soldiers with magnetic grapples ready.

Reinhart's blaster wavered—toward the Council members sitting shocked in their seats, and toward Margaret Duffe, straight at her blue eyes. Reinhart's features were distorted with insane fear. "Get back! Don't anybody come near me or she'll be the first to get it!"

Peter Sherikov slid from the table and with one great stride swept his immense bulk in front of Reinhart. His huge black-furred fist rose in a smashing arc. Reinhart sailed against the wall, struck with ringing force and then slid slowly to the floor.

The Government troops threw their grapples quickly around him and jerked him to his feet. His body was frozen rigid. Blood dripped from his mouth. He spat bits of tooth, his eyes glazed over. Dixon stood dazed, mouth open, uncomprehending, as the grapples closed around his arms and legs.

Reinhart's gun skidded to the floor as he was yanked toward the door. One of the elderly Council members picked the gun up and examined it curiously. He laid it carefully on the table. "Fully loaded," he murmured. "Ready to fire."

Reinhart's battered face was dark with hate. "I should have killed all of you. *All* of you!" An ugly sneer twisted across his shredded lips. "If I could get my hands loose—"

"You won't," Margaret Duffe said. "You might as well not even bother to think about it." She signaled to the troops and they pulled Reinhart and Dixon roughly out of the room, two dazed figures, snarling and resentful.

For a moment the room was silent. Then the Council members shuffled nervously in their seats, beginning to breathe again.

Sherikov came over and put his big paw on Margaret Duffe's shoulder. "Are you all right, Margaret?"

She smiled faintly. "I'm fine. Thanks...."

Sherikov touched her soft hair briefly. Then he broke away and began to pack up his briefcase busily. "I have to go. I'll get in touch with you later."

"Where are you going?" she asked hesitantly. "Can't you stay and—"

"I have to get back to the Urals." Sherikov grinned at her over his bushy black beard as he headed out of the room. "Some very important business to attend to."

Thomas Cole was sitting up in bed when Sherikov came to the door. Most of his awkward, hunched-over body was sealed in a thin envelope of transparent airproof plastic. Two robot attendants whirred ceaselessly at his side, their leads contacting his pulse, blood-pressure, respiration, body temperature.

Cole turned a little as the huge Pole tossed down his briefcase and seated himself on the window ledge.

"How are you feeling?" Sherikov asked him.

"Better."

"You see we've quite advanced therapy. Your burns should be healed in a few months."

"How is the war coming?"

"The war is over."

Cole's lips moved. "Icarus—"

"Icarus went as expected. As *you* expected." Sherikov leaned toward the bed. "Cole, I promised you something. I mean to keep my promise—as soon as you're well enough."

"To return me to my own time?"

"That's right. It's a relatively simple matter, now that Reinhart has been removed from power. You'll be back home again, back in your own time, your own world. We can supply you with some discs of platinum or something of the kind to finance your business. You'll need a new Fixit truck. Tools. And clothes. A few thousand dollars ought to do it."

Cole was silent.

"I've already contacted histo-research," Sherikov continued. "The time bubble is ready as soon as you are. We're somewhat beholden to you, as you probably realize. You've made it possible for us to actualize our greatest dream. The whole planet is seething with excitement. We're changing our economy over from war to—"

"They don't resent what happened? The dud must have made an awful lot of people feel downright bad."

"At first. But they got over it—as soon as they understood what was ahead. Too bad you won't be here to see it, Cole. A whole world breaking loose. Bursting out into the universe. They want me to have an faster-than-light ship ready by the end of the week! Thousands of applications are already on file, men and women wanting to get in on the initial flight."

Cole smiled a little, "There won't be any band, there. No parade or welcoming committee waiting for them."

"Maybe not. Maybe the first ship will wind up on some dead world, nothing but sand and dried salt. But everybody wants to go. It's almost like a holiday. People running around and shouting and throwing things in the streets.

"Afraid I must get back to the labs. Lots of reconstruction work being started." Sherikov dug into his bulging briefcase. "By the way.... One little thing. While you're recovering here, you might like to look at these." He tossed a handful of schematics on the bed.

Cole picked them up slowly. "What's this?"

"Just a little thing I designed." Sherikov arose and lumbered toward the door. "We're realigning our political structure to eliminate any recurrence of the Reinhart affair. This will block any more one-man power grabs." He jabbed a thick finger at the schematics. "It'll turn power over to all of us, not to just a limited number one person could dominate—the way Reinhart dominated the Council.

"This gimmick makes it possible for citizens to raise and decide issues directly. They won't have to wait for the Council to verbalize a measure. Any citizen can transmit his will with one of these, make his needs register on a central control that automatically responds. When a large enough segment of the population wants a certain thing done, these little gadgets set up an active field that touches all the others. An issue won't have to go through a formal Council. The citizens can express their will long before any bunch of gray-haired old men could get around to it."

Sherikov broke off, frowning.

"Of course," he continued slowly, "there's one little detail...."

"What's that?"

"I haven't been able to get a model to function. A few bugs.... Such intricate work never was in my line." He paused at the door. "Well, I hope I'll see you again before you go. Maybe if you feel well enough later on we could get together for one last talk. Maybe have dinner together sometime. Eh?"

But Thomas Cole wasn't listening. He was bent over the schematics, an intense frown on his weathered face. His long fingers moved restlessly over the schematics, tracing wiring and terminals. His lips moved as he calculated.

Sherikov waited a moment. Then he stepped out into the hall and softly closed the door after him.

He whistled merrily as he strode off down the corridor.

THE END